Lament for Darley Dene

Lament for Darley Dene

Stuart G. Yates

Also by Stuart G. Yates

- Unflinching
- In The Blood
- To Die in Glory
- Varangian
- Varangian 2 (King of the Norse)
- Burnt Offerings
- Whipped Up
- Splintered Ice
- The Sandman Cometh
- Roadkill
- Tears in the Fabric of Time
- Sallowed Blood

To Mum, who told me the story, and to Mike who would have loved to have read it.

I miss you both.

Author's Foreword

The story of Darley Dene and what happened there became part of the folklore of my birthplace half a century ago. My mother first told me the story when I was young and I remember thinking then how 'spooky' it was. I doubt, however, if there is anyone left now in my hometown who recalls the tale in any great detail. I know people have memories of the area and amateur historians have tried to gather together bits of evidence, but hardly anyone speaks of the army camp that once stood next to the sprawl of the Birkenhead Docks. If there is anyone who remembers, and you get the chance to speak to them, never forget that it is a factual story, although what you read here is a work of fiction. Nevertheless, elements are true; all you have to do, as reader, is decide which elements are real. However, one important thing is. Men died there in the dreadful early Blitz of the Second World War. Now, some sixty years or so after the event, Darley Dene no longer exists, bulldozed over to make way for the Mersey tunnel approach road. How many drivers, I wonder, know the history of the area across which they are travelling as they make their way to and from the Liverpool Kingsway Tunnel? And if they did, would they pull over, get out of their cars and bow their heads in a moment of quiet respect? Perhaps you, dear reader, will do so if you ever visit Darley Dene.

A Memory Shared

The moment Uncle Ben opened the door and let Henry in, he could see straight away how vulnerable his nephew was feeling. With head hanging down, the young boy shuffled along the hallway, a small, hunted animal surrendering to its fate. Mum and Dad hadn't told him why they had to go away, that much was obvious. And so typical. Too busy with their own lives to worry about their son. Ben caught sight of a concerned face pressed against the car passenger window at the kerbside and, as the vehicle sped off, he raised his hand limply. He was here, to save them from too much worry, to ease Henry's pain…and that was fairly typical too.

Ben helped Henry with his coat. No words broke the depressed atmosphere settling between them and Henry sat and watched the television whilst Ben prepared dinner. They'd asked him to do that too. A terse phone call, a splutter of garbled words. Ben grunted, accepting their pleas for help. There was no one else. Could he look after Henry, just for a few hours … *please*?

Later on, after the main course, Henry moved his spoon around the bowl without actually eating any of the dessert Uncle Ben placed in front of him. He appeared deep in thought. Uncle Ben, noticing his mood, sighed and looked meaningfully at his nephew. "Sorry I don't seem too talkative. I'm not really used to this," he said.

Henry put down his spoon quietly and looked at his Uncle, the slight expression of pain still on his face. "It's not that." He sat back in his chair. "What's happening, Uncle Ben? Why did Mum and Dad drop me off here, without a word? Has someone died?"

Uncle Ben blinked, coughed, shifted position in his chair. "How old are you again?"

"Twelve. What's that got to do with anything?" "Perceptive. For a twelve year old."

"Per-what?"

"Perceptive, means you can guess things really well."

"So, I am right, about someone dying?"

"Well, not quite, no."

Uncle Ben stood up, gathering together the untouched bowl and spoon from in front of Henry. "Your Mum is very upset, Henry. So upset she didn't know what to say. Dad didn't know either. It's Grandpa Frank. He's not very well. Your Mum thought he was getting better, but that's not quite the case."

He paused and for a moment struggled to find the right words. His voice sounded low and heavy when he continued. "We all thought he was getting better. He was in what the doctors call remission. But the chemo has destroyed his body's ability to defend itself and he's caught some sort of infection..." He shrugged his shoulders and went over to the sink with the dishes. "Your Mum didn't want you to see him the way he is right now. That's why you're here whilst your Mum and Dad go and..." His voice trailed away and he began to wash the dishes in the sink. "It'll only be for a few days."

"But they could have told me that themselves, Uncle Ben. Why didn't they? What are they afraid of?"

Uncle Ben gave a little laugh. "Well, I suppose they were thinking of you, thinking you might be frightened... or upset. Which, I suppose you're going to be, Henry."

Henry's face remained blank, his uncle's words filtering through. "Yes, I like Grandpa Frank. I haven't seen much of him lately and now I know why, but..." Henry moved his finger around a little spot of custard that had dribbled down from his bowl, "You see, the thing is, Mum and Dad, they're always like that. Always worried, or scared about what I'll see, or do. They never, ever let me do anything by my-self. All my other mates get to go to the city, go down to the skateboard park, stuff like that. Not me. And now this. It's just not…God, I wish I was older. Fifteen or – or eighteen."

Uncle Ben came back to the table and sat down. He poured Henry a glass of juice and slid it across the table. "Yes, I know. Amazing as it may sound, I used to be twelve once – many years ago."

"I bet your mum let you out to play, didn't she."

Uncle Ben shrugged again. "At first." Ben frowned, "Is that what's really troubling you, that your Mum doesn't trust you enough to let you go out on your own? Your Mum's just afraid, Henry, afraid of lots of things. And this business with her own dad, well it's sort of made you even more precious to her. So that's probably why she's over-protective right now."

"But she always is. When you were twelve, your mum let you out, you said?"

"It's not so simple – the world was different then. Safer. Not so many cars." He smiled at the memory. "But yes, she did let me out on my own. I'd always be in the street, kicking a ball, or playing hide and seek. Lots of bike rides and going on adventures. Getting up to all sorts, but all of it innocent enough. But then – well, like I said, at first she let me do those things, then it all got very scary." He stood up and busied himself with making a cup of coffee, sensing Henry's eyes boring into his back. Struggling to keep the emotion at bay, he cleared his throat noisily and pressed the back of his hand into his eye, hoping against hope his nephew hadn't noticed.

"So, what happened back then, Uncle Ben? What was it that was so scary?"

Ben held onto the edge of the sink and took a deep breath. Henry was more of a terrier than he'd bargained for. He turned to look at him. Was this the right course to follow, he wondered to himself. Reveal-ing things from the past was always fraught with danger and open to misunderstandings. The world was changing with frightening speed and young people … Well, they wanted everything *now*. Instant. A peek into the past might not solve anything at all, might even make things worse. But then, as Ben studied his nephew, he saw the pain, the confusion and he reached a decision. If he could teach Henry a little about how to come to terms with life, the way it can change, the way loss somehow makes you feel stronger, more *equipped* to face life's challenges, then it might just do some good.

He took another deep, ragged breath. This was going to be an emotional journey, raking up long forgotten events. But if it really could help… "Okay," said Uncle Ben emphatically, "I think you could do with a good story. It's long, but it's true. And it's all about being twelve, because when I was twelve something happened to me that was to change my life forever. I didn't know it at the time, of course, because being twelve, well, you just meet things head on, without thinking."

"I try to think, to be sensible, but it isn't easy."

"No. Of course it isn't." He sighed. "So, this story of mine, do you want to hear it?"

Henry gave a single nod and his eyes widened in gleeful expectation. "You bet."

Uncle Ben smiled warmly, "Well, let's go into the living room and sit by the fire with our drinks and I'll tell you my story about Darley Dene."

Chapter One

It was the beginning of one of those glorious summer holidays of long, long ago, the type which seemed to go on and on forever. Ben, no doubt like everyone else of his age, had plenty of ambitions for the school break. School was over for seven glorious weeks – *seven weeks.* A lifetime when you're only twelve. Try as he might, he couldn't really remember previous summer breaks. Not that he tried very hard, there was no point – why try and remember the past? It was gone, done and dusted. But one thing he did recall – nothing much *ever* happened. So this time would be different. This was going to be the first year when he actually felt determined to do something memorable, something new. Perhaps it was an indication that he was growing up, becoming a young adult, which made him more single-minded. A holiday, how-ever short or long, was an opportunity for exploration, to experience. He certainly found himself wanting to know more about life now. He'd read books for hours, stare out of his window just thinking, looking forward to the weekends when he could wander up to the park, dis-covering new types of flowers, or trees, or birds. He'd often go to the library – if his mates found out, they'd rib him forever – and he'd read up about gorillas, tigers, killer whales. The world was opening up its treasures for him, and it was a chest stuffed full with wondrous delights. So, he made himself a mental checklist of all the things he'd like to accomplish during that long hot summer.

He'd like to improve his swimming, learn to kick a football properly, climb 'Granny's Rock' for the first time... so much to do and look forward to. He stared up at his ceiling and let out a long, contented sigh. Seven weeks. What a thought that was.

He turned over and wallowed in the self-satisfied knowledge that despite there being so much to look forward to, for now, on this first day, the plan was to do nothing but lie-in until eleven or even twelve noon. There was going to be plenty of time for all that other stuff. He had to be careful though. His Mum got in from work at quarter-past twelve, and if she were to catch Ben in bed at that time there would be hell to pay. This proved a little disconcerting as he lay all snug underneath his bed-clothes, because he didn't know what time it was. He yawned, stretched and reluctantly dragged himself from the warmth of his bed, reached for his jeans and t-shirt and pulled them on.

Most days Trevor would call round. Ben had first met Trevor more than eight years ago. On that fateful morning, whilst playing at the bottom of the alleyway that ran along the back of his house, Ben had seen Trevor for the first time. Ben´s mum told him never to cross the road at the bottom of the alleyway. It was forbidden, she said through gritted teeth. Ben never really knew why she seemed so concerned and this lent the road, and what might lie beyond, an almost mystical air. Across the tarmac was a fabled world, mysterious and unlike his own – of big houses with private driveways and lush gardens. Whereas Ben's house was a tiny, rented terrace, the houses on the other side were privately owned. They stood proud and strong, majestic mansions of old. Red-bricked, gabled roofs, ornamental front gardens that led to enormous entrance-ways out of which prim and proper people emerged, resplendent in expensive and fashionable clothes. Some even drove motor cars. From where did the money come for such luxuries, he often wondered. To Ben, across that narrow sliver of tarmac, a different world existed, one ripe for exploration. Perhaps that was the reason for his mum's command not to wander there. Whatever the truth, many a day he sat astride his trike and gazed longingly towards that unattainable land, letting his imagination fill in the gaps.

On that particular day, so long ago, as Ben peddled up and down on his trike with his usual enthusiasm, he'd spotted a shorthaired little boy on the other side, riding a two-wheel bicycle with a confident, almost arrogant ease. Ben stopped and stared in awe, eyes wide, mouth hanging open in disbelief. This new boy couldn't have been any older than him, sat astride a real bike – and without stabilizers! Emerging from one of those big houses, his well-scrubbed face and newly-pressed clothes spoke of parents who cared and had money to spend – mirrored in the gleaming newness of his bike as he rode up and down the pavement on the far side of the forbidden road.

He stopped all of a sudden, this sparkling boy, and stared directly towards Ben. A ghost of a smile crossed his face and Bern´s hand came up as if on its own volition. The stranger called over a greeting and the two struck up a conversation, shouting across to each other from opposite sides of the tarmac. It seemed so effortless, so easy, as if their friendship was already years old. They had so much in common, despite their obvious differences in wealth and privilege and from that point on they had become firm friends. Mum was approached and, after much pleading and begging, she allowed Ben to visit Trevor's house, which turned out to be a vast and sumptuous residence, with vaulted ceilings, wide corridors and rooms big enough, it seemed to Ben, to hold a herd of elephants. To rear sprawled a large garden with steps wending their way down to a little gate, a gate, Trevor explained, which always remained locked. Beyond, down another path, was a railway siding.

"Should we climb over?" asked Ben one day, checking first that no adults loomed close by.

"I'm not supposed to," said Trevor, downcast, a little embarrassed.

"No one will know."

A silent agreement, Trevor's eyes alive with expectation, and they climbed over the gate and entered a new world full of adventure and wonder. And, unlike the vagueness of the world 'across the road', this one proved truly wondrous.

The years went by and their friendship developed. True, like boys the world over, they'd had their arguments, their fights but they'd always made up again. Now, with the school holidays stretching ahead of them, Trevor first told Ben about Darley Dene.

"There's this bigger boy, lives a few doors down from me. His name's Neville. He went there a few days ago, with a gang of others and they'd discovered a whole network of tunnels and caves just begging to be explored. He thought I might like to go and I said yes."

"You said yes?"

"It'll be a laugh," said Trevor enthusiastically, as he sat opposite Ben at the kitchen table.

Ben tucked into a huge bowl of cereal, savouring every delicious mouthful as if he hadn't eaten for days. As he munched down another huge spoonful, he eyed Trevor harshly. "I know Neville."

"You know him? As a friend you mean?"

"Do me a favour, Trev. I know him from school. He's a year above me, like I'm a year above you. He got hold of me once, around the throat, said I was a whinger, a tell-tale, that my mum couldn't afford to buy me proper school shoes. All the usual stuff. He's a bully. He hates me and I hate him."

"All the girls like him," said Trevor, his eyes staring out into the distance. "They all hang around him in the playground, their eyes all dreamy, giggling pathetically whenever he makes some stupid remark, or farts."

"He makes me sick."

"He's not all bad, Ben."

"To you maybe, but I think it's because I have a poor home life that he hates me so much, why he calls me a snivelling weed. I don't know and I don't care."

"I know he can be a bit – you know, *dangerous.* I've seen him in fights."

"Yeah, and I've been on the end of it, him grabbing me, breathing his stinking breath all over me, telling me to give him all my money.

There's a laugh – he has a go at me for not having good shoes, then he demands money. He's pathetic."

"Yeah, but you've stood up to him."

"And got a slap across the face for it – more than once too." He looked down at the remains of his cereal and pushed the bowl away, sighing. "I'm not going if he's there."

Trevor leaned across and touched Ben's arm, his eyes wide, pleading. "Paul will be there as well."

Ben stared, twisting his mouth around, a little of the tension leaving his body. Paul was the total opposite to Neville. Kind, patient, clever, everyone at school looked up to him, treating him like some sort of hero. And Ben was no different. He knew the influence Paul had on Neville. Whenever he was around, Neville always refrained from his usual bullying. Victims always felt much safer whenever Paul was close by. The problem was, with his mum and dad splitting up, he usually kept himself to himself during any free time away from school. "Isn't he with his dad?"

"We're all on holiday, and his dad's at work all day," said Trevor, "so he's with his mum most of the time."

Nodding, Ben caught the eagerness in Trevor's eyes and smiled. "Well, if Paul's there, I will be too."

Trevor gave a little whoop of delight and sprang to his feet. He delved into a cupboard under the sink and brought out a bottle of green cream soda, which he poured into two tumblers. He handed one across to his friend.

"So, it's just a load of twisting tunnels?" asked Ben, closing his eyes as the many tiny bubbles of gas sprang up from the glass and exploded on his face.

"You don't think that's exciting?" Trevor shook his head, looking sad that his friend was being so serious, perhaps even dull.

Ben drank and shrugged, "No, it's not that. But there's got to be something else there, hasn't there? To make it exciting. Where is it, and why's it called 'Darley Dene'?"

"Down the hill, and I don't know why it's called that, it just is. Why do you always have to get so boring about stuff? You always need to know all the details about everything."

"I just like to know reasons, that's all. Like why Neville hates me so much."

"God, Ben, not that again! Isn't it obvious? For the same reasons you hate him."

"Why, because I've got a brain the size of a newt and I love smacking people in the face?"

"Don't be stupid." He took a deep breath and when he continued, his voice was low, serious. "It's because you're clever and he's not. I heard all about it. He's jealous of you."

"Jealous? Of me? Don't make me laugh."

"It's true – he told me."

"He told you?"

"He was put down a year, wasn't he – and who did he sit next to in class? You. And there you were, answering all the questions as if they were the easiest thing in the world."

"God, is that what all this is about?" He blew out his breath, exasperated. "Trev, I can't help it if I'm good at maths and English. It's not my fault is it?"

"No, it's not your fault, but you could have handled it a bit better. Maybe helped him."

"I didn't know why he was put down. He just appeared one day in our class, and I never asked him. He was so big, so ... *intimidating*." He shrugged again. "Anyway, I tried, I really did, Trev. I tried to show him how to do things, but he just got angry."

"And then you laughed at him, didn't you, Ben? He told me, after that first day. We were walking home and he told me you laughed when he got something wrong."

"I...I didn't mean to laugh at him. It was such a simple question – which was the biggest island in the world before Australia was discovered. He just looked at Mr. Woods and sort of gave up. Shrugged his shoulders."

"So why did you laugh?"

"I wasn't the only one."

"Well, maybe you weren't, but then you go and shout out the answer, before he's even had a chance to think about it." Trevor closed his eyes. "You're different with him, Ben, and you don't even know it. It's almost as if you don't like him because you think he's thick."

"That's not true."

"It's what *he* thinks. He thinks you make fun of him, so he gets angry. But, like I said, the main thing is – he's jealous."

"Jealous? So, he beats me up because he's jealous of me being clever? Great…I thought maybe it was because he's twice the size of me and loves to see me cry."

Trevor sat back in his chair. "I like you Ben, and you're my friend, so I'll tell you what you need to do – you have to stand up to Neville more often, tell him how you feel and, if that doesn't work, tell him exactly what you think of *him*."

Ben gave a short laugh. "I already tried that," he said, "and I got a punch in the nose for my efforts." He shook his head. "But if Paul is going, then things should be all right."

"Yeah, and Paul wouldn't be going if it wasn't really interesting, would he? Paul is exactly like you, only older."

"And about ten times bigger. Bigger than Neville at least. That's what it's all about, you know. When you think about it, all that really matters is how big you are. It doesn't matter if you're clever, it's not going to help you in a fight. I think I'm going to send away for that 'Charles Atlas' thing and develop a superhuman body."

Trevor frowned at him for a moment, then burst into laughter, "Yeah, then you can hit him on the knee with your nose!"

"Or smack my eye into his fist." They both screamed at this.

In between bouts of laughter, they hatched a plan and set off, like intrepid explorers, down the winding path. As they tramped along, Ben realized Trevor hadn't answered any of his questions about where they were going, but felt sure nothing would remain a mystery for long. As they neared 'Darley Dene', unbeknownst to Ben, more than the meaning and origins of its name awaited discovery. Soon, he would know the true meaning of terror.

Chapter Two

He felt his throat tighten as his biggest fear loomed up ahead of him. Standing there, with that ape-like grin splitting his face, chin jutting forward, fists planted provocatively on his hips, was Neville Federman, Ben's nemesis. Already laughing as Ben scrambled over the wall separating Darley Dene from the road, Neville turned to the other assembled boys busy building a fire.

"Hey you lot, look who it is." He turned his gloating face to Ben once again, "It's the wimp. Hiya wimp, come to help us with our fire? We could use some help, wimp, so why don't you come over here and I'll set fire to yer head."

Neville laughed at what he thought was an incredibly witty joke, laughed so much he almost choked. Whilst he bent double and coughed hoarsely, Ben simply strode past him, not giving him so much as a cursory glance.

If he hoped to quieten the bully by this show of ignorance, Ben was mistaken. No doubt irked that his taunts had brought no reaction, Neville now resorted to a more direct approach, grabbing Ben by the collar and pulling him around roughly.

Without a thought, Ben knocked Neville's hand away and stood, red faced, in front of his tormenter. Trevor, who'd been watching the incident with growing alarm, stepped forward, just as Neville tensed. "Come on, Nev," he said, voice taking on a pleading note, "we've come here for some fun, remember?"

Neville, never taking his eyes off Ben, snarled menacingly, "That's what I'm doing, Trev."

Trevor persisted, "Nev, please, just leave it."

In response, Neville grew more agitated, his voice breaking with anger, "I asked you to come here, Trev, not him," and he punctuated his remark by stabbing a thick finger into Ben's chest.

Ben stood his ground, despite the pain. In fact, it surprised him how much that single finger hurt him. He resisted the urge to rub the tender spot and narrowed his eyes to prevent them from watering. He wasn't about to show the bully what pain he'd caused with just a finger.

Then a voice of reason, a voice that could not be argued against, came to them and a tremendous sense of relief rushed through him. Paul, big and burly, sauntered up to the little group and declared softly, "I asked him to come, Neville. Now leave him alone."

For a moment there was a chance that Neville might argue, but it passed and a collective sigh escaped from the others. With a face paralyzed with rage, Neville stomped off, leaving Paul to place a friendly hand on Ben's shoulder. "He's not so bad, really."

"You think?" Ben rubbed his chest furiously, wincing as he did so, "He's a bully and one day I'm going to punch him back."

Paul raised a single eyebrow. "That would be good to see. But don't let him worry you too much, not today anyway – we've got lots to explore."

And still holding him by the shoulder, Paul led Ben towards the rest of the gang, introducing them one by one. Ben glanced back to see Trevor watching them. There was a look of unease about him. Was there going to be trouble, Ben wondered. Neville was not the sort to back down with any grace. He'd find a way of reaping revenge, of that Ben was certain. He was also certain that there wouldn't be anything anyone, Trevor or Paul included, could do about it. The realization left him feeling trapped and a little nervous, ringing his hands, eyes forever darting towards Neville who paced around like a caged beast, ready to spring forward at any moment. So much for having fun, Ben mused.

Throughout the long morning and into the afternoon they played, nine of them altogether. The surrounding area was sparse, the soil an insipid yellow colour. Nothing much grew here except for the rim of trees, which formed a natural barrier between where they played and the thick undergrowth beyond. A little stream ran through the wasteland and here they built a stepping stone bridge to transport them across to the other side. Once across, through the trees and over the rise, an expanse of marshland stretched out far into the distance. Punctuating the view, a latticework of railways tracks, glinting in the sunlight, led to a large marshalling yard. From here came the sound of steam locomotives, straining to haul their loads, great grey plumes of steam and smoke emanating from their funnels, spiralled upwards to smudge across the blue background of sky. Nearby stood Spraggs' Farm, with people, tiny dots amongst the landscape. A place of mystery, one that Ben had never seen before, had no idea even existed. He felt Paul at his shoulder and turned and smiled up at his friend.

"They bombed all of this, in the War," Paul explained, without any preamble. "I can barely remember it. A few bangs, noises… the only thing that really sticks in my mind is a great big flash in my room. We didn't have a shelter and, as far as I know, the whole thing took us all by surprise. Mum told me, ages later, that an incendiary came through my window and landed on the dresser. She had to rush in and smother it with a blanket."

"What's an incendiary?"

"Sort of stick bomb. The Germans dropped thousands of 'em. Like long, silver sticks. They used to go up in flames a few seconds after they hit the ground, burning everything around them. I was lucky…thanks to my Mum."

Ben gave a deep smile. His Mum rarely spoke about the War, the memories perhaps too painful. All he had were scraps, torn fragments of jumbled up conversations, whispered narratives of a time best left behind. He knew his Dad had fallen in the War, but he didn't know how, or when. An incident he felt he couldn't, or shouldn't, ask about, despite believing he had a right to know. His Dad was a shadowy figure, and if he ever thought about him, he was nothing more than a distant, unformed figure, lost in the darkness. Perhaps when he was older, he might ask his Mum for a photograph. Details. For now, her moods so changeable, he kept such questions to himself.

"Come on," said Paul, cutting into Ben's reverie, his tone changing from morose to excited, "we better go and do your initiation."

"My what?"

Paul grinned. "Come on – you'll see."

Parts of the stream branched off into tiny tributaries or ponds. At one of these, the boys had managed to suspend a swing rope from the branch of an over-hanging tree.

"This is all part of the initiation," Paul said, holding onto the thick rope, grinning at Ben. "All new members of the gang have to go through it – you're no exception. You have to swing across to the other side, in one go. If you fail, you'll either fall in, or, if you don't, we'll push you into that filthy stinking water, fully clothed."

Ben bit his bottom lip, looking from the rope, then across the water to the far side. It seemed an impossible task, the other bank so far away it might as well be on the other side of the Atlantic. "Has anyone failed?"

"Up until now," said Paul, "three have. Two of them ran off like little cry-babies, but one tried again and got through." He smiled. "Trevor."

"Trevor failed it?" Ben rubbed his hand over his face, "If he failed, I don't think I've got any chance."

"You're not listening – he tried again, and got through."

"So, I can have another go?"

Paul shrugged. "There is another test, but I'm not going to tell you what that is – and neither is Trev. It's a secret." He thrust the rope towards Ben. "Don't think about any of that – just concentrate on getting across. Take a deep breath, run backwards and then give it all you've got."

Ben stared at the rope, struggling with the idea of failure, and its consequences. It might be better to just turn around and run back home. Then a voice cut through his thoughts.

"He won't do it, the wimp!" shouted Neville from the other side, head back, mouth open, laughing so loudly his body shook.

Next to him, Trevor pulled a face then smiled across to Ben. "I think you'll be surprised, Nev. Ben's tougher than he looks." He winked and Ben grew easier. Perhaps he could do it after all. Sucking in his breath, he stared across. What was the distance? Ten feet? If he ran hard enough, there might be a chance ...

"Never!" said Neville, his voice mocking. He sneered. "He's just a wimp. You're a wimp, isn't that right, you Nancy-boy!"

Ignoring the jibes, Ben looked from the rope, to Paul and back again. It hung there, rough and thick, barely moving in the breeze. He would have to launch himself off the bank with every ounce of effort and swing across to the other side like Tarzan if he was to have any sort of chance.

"It's not going to be easy," said Paul, voice low but strangely comforting. "You're not that big, so you'll have to put all of your strength into the initial leap."

"I have to do it," said Ben. He spat into his hands. "I can't let him win, can I?"

Paul smiled. "No. You can't."

Taking a firm hold of the rope, Ben took a few steps backwards and, after one, last glance towards Paul, he charged forward.

They were all sitting around the camp-fire, roasting potatoes in the flames. Everyone, that is, except Neville, who stomped around the periphery of the group kicking the ground, mouth downturned, sullen, Since Ben's dramatic success in swinging over the murky water, Neville dared not match anyone's stare. Eventually, sulking, he wandered over to a fallen tree trunk some way off, tugged out a penknife, and took to whittling away at a gnarled piece of wood he'd found. No-one spoke to him, nor paid him any mind.

Ben sat with the others, basking in their congratulations, many of them back-slapping him. Paul nodded, impressed, and Trevor beamed, punching his friend playfully on the arm. "I knew you could do it," he said.

Some moments later, Neville returned, sauntering over to the group, the merest flicker of a smile playing around the corners of his mouth. He flopped down next to Ben and clapped him on the shoulder.

"Well done Ben."

A gasp came from out of everyone's mouth, except for Ben, who simply stared at his tormentor. "Thanks," he said, voice even, emotionless.

Neville shrugged, "I have to say, that was a really good jump. You must have been practicing."

"No. First time I've done it."

"Really? Well, that's even more amazing. You're part of the gang now, Benny-boy." Chuckling, he looked down at the piece of wood in his hand. "I'm sorry, but, you know what, I wasn't really looking when you did your jump…actually, I failed at mine." Ben caught a surprised look from Paul. Could the bully have changed so quickly? Paul shrugged. No one else spoke. "So, I was wondering, seeing as you're pretty good, would you do it again, so I can…learn something?"

Paul spoke up, "You don't have to do that, Ben. You passed, you're in the gang."

"Of course he is," declared Neville, grinning now, "we all know that, but I'd really like to see it. Not as a test, it's just that I wasn't really watching him. I want to see how he did it."

Paul stared. "It's up to you Ben. Just do it like before – a big run, then swing with all your might."

And it was like before. Ben raced forward, grunting with the effort, and sailed across, shifting his weight forward, swinging out into mid-air.

But then it all changed.

Almost as soon as his feet left the bank, Ben felt the rope weakening. No longer rough and strong, the fibres parted until, with a loud crack like a gunshot, the improvised swing snapped and he fell, the world tumbling around him in a mad cascade of images and colours. As if in slow-motion, he saw himself plunging towards the pond, and he knew, with awful certainty, there was nothing he could do to stop himself. He cried out as he hit the thick, stinking brown water with a resounding splash, and at that moment, he understood everything.

Sitting forlornly amidst water with the consistency of thick, melted chocolate oozing into his shoes, his shirt, his underwear, he sat and closed his eyes with shame as raucous laughter broke out from the on-lookers. And, in the centre of them, Neville's roaring, maniacal cackle, gloating over Ben's failure.

He sensed a movement close by and looked up to see Neville's fat, greasy face, jutting forward, his great mouth gaping open, the foul words spilling out, "Unlucky, wimpy, unlucky." Behind him, the gang, all of them bent double, waggling their fingers, consumed with glee. Ben looked at each face in turn. Standing a little way off was Paul, his face impassive, and Trevor, his friend. He seemed to be in conflict, his mouth chewed up as if in pain, struggling with uncertainty, a desire to … what, help?

But nobody offered to help him clamber out of the sucking, stinking pond. With the gloop dripping in great globules from his clothes, Ben slowly got to his feet. Ignoring the laughter, he gazed at the piece of rope in his hand, the piece of rope he had grabbed on to, which had snapped almost as soon as he swung out across the space between the two banks, the piece of rope which he knew for sure had been cut by Neville's knife.

Chapter Three

With the taunts and the jeers ringing in his ears, Ben trudged off towards the wall separating Darley Dene from the road beyond. Caked in thick sludge, he moved along, head down, wishing he was already home, hidden away beneath the blankets of his bed. The mud dried quickly, but not in the places that mattered, and his thoughts turned to Mum and what she would say when she saw him, so dirty, his clothes ruined. He shuddered at the prospect.

As he neared the wall, his foot struck something hard. He cursed and looked down, half expecting to see a boulder, but instead saw a round, metal shape, red with rust, poking out from the compacted earth. Curious, he bent down, dusting away the soil covering the top of it. He wriggled his fingers into the dirt, got them under the object and heaved it out into the daylight.

Holding it up like a trophy, he gasped.

It was a steel helmet, as worn by British soldiers of the Second World War. Although rusted on the crown, the rest appeared in remarkably good condition, its leather liner intact. Turning it over, he read an embossed inscription, bearing the date '1938'. Ben didn't know very much about history, but he knew the War broke out in 1939, meaning the issue date placed this helmet in the period before war broke out. But why it slept here, buried in the ground for sixteen years, he couldn't think. Perhaps a soldier, based in the camp, had dropped it accidentally and forgotten all about it. Such a scenario didn't make much sense, for the trouble he'd have received from his company sergeant would have forced the poor man to search until he found it.

Studying it, Ben's mind painted pictures of war-time training, of men racing across obstacle courses, bayonetting straw-filled bags, live-round target practise, unarmed combat … He licked his lips, recalling the old recruiting films he often watched at the cinema. Such a great time to be alive, to experience the adventure, the thrill of marching off and fighting in the War.

Sighing, Ben looped his arm through the chinstrap and clambered over the wall, making short work of the climb, before dropping down on the other side.

He made his way home, dragging his feet, feeling like a complete fool. People milling around, talking on doorsteps, stared with bemused expressions, wondering why a small, bedraggled boy covered in mud was traipsing through the streets. To them, he must have looked like a creature from the black lagoon. Doing his best to ignore the giggles and the muttered questions, he trundled on, head down, until he reached his front door.

He paused for a moment, thinking what he needed to say. Nan would be home and as soon as she saw the state of him, she'd demand an explanation. Should he come up with some tall tale, or should he tell the truth and take the consequences? Nan was not the sort of person to meddle with; if she found out he was lying, he'd get a cuff round the ear for sure.

Reaching his decision, he pressed the doorbell and waited.

She stood, in the doorway, her face a perfect mask of neutrality. Without a word, she stepped aside, beckoning him into the kitchen where he pulled off his shoes and dirty clothes. Nan took them and put them straight into the bucket by the sink. She stomped upstairs and he heard the squeal of taps turning, of water pumping into the bath.

The water felt good, almost luxuriant, as he slipped down beneath the warm sea of foam that Nan prepared for him. As he lay back, he could hear her busying herself downstairs, preparing his caked clothes for washing. Then the sound of her feet, ascending the stairs. He read-ied himself, sitting up, knees pressed against his chest, face down.

The door wheezed open and there she stood, arms folded, face stern, eyes unblinking.

"I think you need to explain."

And she waited and he knew there was no place to run to, no chance to weave a story. She'd pick through every stitch, recognizing every falsehood. He took a breath, turning his face towards her, but only slightly. "I went down to Darley Dene."

"Is that where this helmet came from?"

He turned to see it in her hand. He nodded.

"You found it?"

"It was half buried."

"And what made you bring it home?"

"I don't know. A feeling. I thought I might clean it up, hang it on the wall of something."

"Oh, you did, did you?"

"Yes. Why, have I done something wrong?"

She bit her lip then, allowing her eyes to roam across the pitted but otherwise perfect wartime helmet. "Don't tell your mother," she said at last and went out.

Ben's eyes rested on the open doorway where she had stood, won-dering why she had told him not to say anything more. What was it about the mention of Darley Dene that seemed to cause such fear, anguish and anger? He couldn't think which one it might be worse, perhaps a mixture of all three. Whatever, it was curious, and the way she looked at the helmet with that faraway, distant look in her eye. He couldn't fathom it, not then, and not throughout the next few hours.

After he dried and dressed himself in crisp, clean clothes, he mooched around his room, trying to find something to take his mind off the developing sense of unease running around inside his head. Nothing held his attention, so at last, unable to contain his patience any longer, he ran down the stairs and went straight into the kitchen, to find Nan about to put his trousers through the mangle. "Nan," he said, "why would Darley Dene upset Mum so much?"

She stopped in the action of turning the mangle's handle and stood, back to him, hunched over the ancient washing machine, her breathing ragged, not with exertion, but with apprehension.

Slowly she turned, taking up a towel to dry her hands, and looked at Ben with a pained expression. "Just let's say that Mum wouldn't be very pleased about you being there."

"Yes, but why wouldn't she?"

"It's dangerous. She'd be worried out of her mind if she knew you were poking around down there."

"Poking around? Dangerous? Nan, you have to tell me – what is it about Darley Dene that makes it so dangerous?"

Her eyebrows rose at this, "Let's just leave it like that." Her voice changed, becoming sharp and angry as she loomed over him, "What have you found down there, apart from that helmet?"

Ben took a step back, shocked at her sudden change of mood. "Nothing else" he said, "I promise." She appeared to relax, some of the red slipping from her face, and she sat down heavily at the kitchen table. Ben leaned towards her. "What is that helmet, Nan? Why was it there?"

For a long time, his Grandmother stared at the tabletop, as if an answer might be found in the stains and scratches of its old, well used surface. Then she looked up, her eyes returning to their usual gentleness. She smiled. "Ben, I can't tell you everything. That wouldn't be right, but I'll tell you some of it. It's not that important, I suppose, but…" She spread out her hands, "That place is not a happy one, Ben. Not a happy one. During the War, it was an army camp. Men stayed there when the threat of invasion was quite serious. You know what an invasion is, don't you? We were terribly afraid back then. No-one knew when the Germans would come, you see, but we felt sure they would. And no-one knew where or how they might come, so we had to be prepared. Paratroopers was what we were told. And that is why the soldiers were camped there, next to the docks, just in case… silly, stupid place to put them really. Don't know why the generals, or whoever it was, decided to put them there." She shook her head. "Putting them at such risk, it was criminal."

"Risk from what, Nan?"

"Bombs. We were being bombed, night after night. The Germans would come, targeting the docks, the factories, the bridges. It was quite awful, Ben. Frightening. We used to shelter under the stairs. We'd put a big mattress up in front of us, so if we got hit, the mattress would fall on us and protect us from the falling bricks. Auntie Kay had seen houses in Liverpool that had been bombed and she always said that the staircases were the only part still standing even though the rest of the house had fallen down. So that's why we sat under there, with the mattress. But we never got hit, thank goodness. Not us..." Her voice trailed away and for a time, Ben stood in silence, waiting, not wanting to speak and so break the spell. He slowly went over to her and put his head on her shoulder. She put her hand against his cheek and patted it softly. "You're a good boy, Ben. That's enough for now. Listen, I know you want to go and play with your friends, but there's things down there...things that I don't want you to see. And Mum would be upset if she thought you'd...found anything."

"But you haven't told me what, Nan, or why."

She sighed deeply, "Oh, Ben...I wish I could, but I can't. It wouldn't be right."

"You already said that, Nan. Not right for who?"

She sat back, pulling him around and placing both her hands on each of his shoulders. She looked him straight in the eyes. "For your Mum, Ben. It wouldn't be right for your Mum. She needs to tell you, in her own time." She closed her eyes, paused for a moment before opening them again. They were moist with the threat of tears. "When she's ready, Ben, she'll tell you. When she's ready."

Chapter Four

Later the same day, Uncle Brendon, Mum's brother, arrived, and asked if Ben would like to go up to Central Park. "They're putting on a military tattoo," he said, "and I thought we could wander around and take a look at the preparations."

Bouncing up and down in front of his mum, Ben stopped when he caught the look on Nan's face. For one awful moment, he thought she might say something, but then Mum ruffled his hair, "Why not. That will be great fun, won't it, Ben?"

"Wow, thanks Mum."

As he went to the door, he paused for a moment, catching Nan's eye again. She gave the briefest of winks, and he stepped outside, unable to contain his delight any longer as he skipped and laughed his way through the streets.

It was a warm, balmy evening. As usual, Uncle Brendon didn't speak very much, but he rarely did, having a cigarette forever stuffed in his mouth like a permanent fixture. Ben liked to think of his uncle as something of a movie-star character. Robert Taylor perhaps; a rugged, outdoor type. But when he caught a whiff of the acrid smoke, his clothes forever impregnated with the smell of stale tobacco, Ben wasn't quite so sure if he'd made the right connection. He wondered if Robert Taylor's breath stank in the same way.

Reaching Central Park, they made their way to the area set aside for all the military personal involved in the tattoo, Ben was surprised not to see a great many more people.

"Memories of the War and, the recent Korean conflict, are still very vivid for a lot of people," explained Uncle Brandon. "It's all a bit raw. There was a rumour that the whole event would be scrapped, but I think they got given a last minute retrieve by the local council."

Ben, grateful for that, couldn't help smiling as he stood and gazed around, wide-eyed, expectant.

Uncle and nephew sauntered through the assembled mass of military hardware, static displays, and the many tents thrown together to form a sort of village. Primarily an army display, with infantry and artillery forming the main focus, there was little room for tanks. "I wanted to see a Sherman," Ben said, trying but failing to keep the disappointment out of his voice.

Uncle Brandon, a sailor in the Royal Navy during the War, gave an apologetic smile. "I'm going to find myself a cup of coffee. Don't wander too far." Lighting up yet another cigarette, he strolled away.

Ben sighed, relieved to be alone and to have the chance to investigate what was going on unhindered.

And there was a lot.

The various tents and sideshows bristled with everything military. Ben, in his element, approached two scary looking M.P.s, who ruffled his hair and let him hold a Sterling submachine gun. Another soldier, whom he thought was some sort of guardsman, allowed him to get down into the dirt and aim along the barrel of a Bren gun. There was even a Bren gun carrier for him to clamber over, pretend to steer, and generally just mess around on. He met Jimmy Baxter, a friend from school whose mother laughed and joked with some of the uniformed men close by, and the two boys played for a while, running in-between tent guy-ropes, very nearly tripping over each other before some burly soldier with two stripes on his arm told them to 'clear off!'

After Jimmy said goodbye and went to rejoin his mother, Ben wandered into a quieter area. Here, filled with an array of cooking utensils, stood several large tents, with display boards detailing life in the Army Catering Corps. Not in the least inspired, Ben eased himself between the tents to an area tucked behind, as if an afterthought. A solitary bivouac stood, with a lonely trestle table outside, covered with various pamphlets. A well dressed young sergeant pored over a text book and, behind him, a sign declared that this was 'Military Intelligence'. Intrigued, Ben stepped up to an information hoarding and studied the few photographs, with their accompanying descriptions. The initials SOE kept on flashing up in almost every sentence.

"Excuse me," Ben said quietly, not taking his eyes off the board, "What's SOE stand for?"

The non-commissioned officer gave a huge sigh. "What?"

Ben turned and saw the scowl of resentment on the man's face. "SOE," he repeated, undaunted, "What's it mean?"

"Special Operations Executive," the soldier replied, in a very bored voice and returned to his book.

Ben continued looking. "Ah," he said, with heavy sarcasm, "I see. Very enlightening." He turned and made as if to go.

Putting down his book, the soldier sat forward, "Just a moment."

Raising a single eyebrow, Ben waited.

"You interested in this sort of stuff then?"

Ben shrugged, "Wouldn't be here if I wasn't, would I?"

Bristling a little, the soldier considered Ben with narrowed eyes. "I suppose not. You here on your own, or with your dad?"

Ben stepped over to the table and picked up one of the leaflets. It showed a soldier in a woolly hat, face smeared with black paint, cutting through some wire fencing with a pair of pliers. "Not my Dad. My Uncle is over by the coffee bar. Why?"

Shrugging, the sergeant gathered several leaflets together and passed them over to Ben. "Just wondering. Most people are interested in Special Ops if their dad, or some other relative, was involved in the War. Was your dad involved in any way?"

Ben, never taking his eyes off the leaflets, shrugged, "I'm not sure. I – I didn't know him."

An awkward silence followed with Ben staring sightlessly at the leaflet, reading the same sentence half a dozen times before he looked up. The soldier studied him intently, as if he were waiting for Ben to continue. Ben sighed. "Mum says he was killed in North Africa."

The soldier nodded, "So, he was a soldier?"

"I don't know many of the details," he said quietly, staring down at his shoes. "I've never asked Mum, not that much, and Nan … Well, it's awkward."

"Awkward? Strange word to use."

"Oh?" Ben shrugged again. "Mum only told me after I punched Terry Peebles for calling my Dad 'yeller-bellied."

"You punched him?"

"Wouldn't you, if someone said that about your dad?"

The soldier held up his hand. "I'm not blaming you, lad. I'd probably feel the same. What happened?"

"I punched the slimy little toad twice and knocked him down. Mr. Forster grabbed me and marched me off to the Head's office. I got four strokes on the backside for that."

"Seems a bit severe. What did this Peebles get?"

"Nothing. I didn't realize what I'd done until the ambulance came into the playground. They took him off to hospital. Later on, the police came to visit me at my house. I was sick. They told me I'd broken Peebles' jaw."

"Must have been a hell of a punch."

"If truth be known, I couldn't give a damn about Peebles, his jaw, or anything else about him. If he ever says anything like it again, I'd do exactly the same."

"Bet your mum was angry."

"At first, but when I finally got up the courage to tell her exactly why it had all happened, she began to cry. Nan came in and we all sat on my bed, and that's when Mum told me a little about Dad."

"About him being killed in Africa?"

"Yes. She told me he'd been a soldier, in a commando unit. He died in North Africa on a raid. But what raid and when, or how he was killed, I haven't a clue. She wouldn't say any more."

He stopped and stared. What invisible power forced him to tell this stranger so much? This wiry soldier, with the beady eyes and immaculate haircut, watched him like a hawk, almost forcing him to say more. But Ben couldn't. He slowly put the leaflet back down on the trestle table.

"A Commando?" Stepping around the table, the soldier stood next to Ben. He tapped his arm, with the three stripes on his shirt. "I'm a sergeant in the Royal Marine Commandoes, you see. It wouldn't be difficult to find out the whole story. If you want to, that is."

Ben looked up, his eyes full of wonder, but the moment went and he shook his head. "What would be the point," he said, voice sounding.

Now it was the sergeant's turn to shrug, "It could answer a few questions."

"Or create a few problems."

"I don't think so. Look, we're here for the next two days. Sunday's the last day. If you change your mind, come and find me again."

"I'll think about it."

"I'll need his name." Ben frowned. "Your dad's name. Full name. It'll help."

"Why?"

The sergeant gave a short laugh, "Because an awful lot of men served and died in North Africa, son."

"What?"

"Thousands of them. Have you ever heard of El Alamein?" He pressed on before Ben could answer, "It would certainly make things easier for me if I had his name."

"You just called me 'son'."

The sergeant stopped, mouth opening slightly. "A figure of speech, nothing more."

Ben studied him. He possessed a latent strength in his well developed frame, like a coiled spring, his shoulders stretching his tunic tight across his back, the muscles bunched and powerful. "But I'm not your son. I'm no man's son."

"I'm sorry, I didn't mean...All right, let's leave it for now. I'll see you on Sunday if you're interested."

Without another word, he turned on his heels and ducked into the tent. Ben sniffed hard and ran the back of his hand across his face. Talking about Dad, reliving that awful day when he dumped Peebles on his skinny behind, brought the tears unchecked to his eyes. He quickly picked up another leaflet, stuffed it into his pocket and stomped off, back to where he thought Uncle Brendon was.

It was growing dark now. People thronged around the various stalls and somewhere in the distance a tannoy made a series of jumbled up announcements. Ben couldn't understand a word. Rising panic welled up inside him. Disorientated, he scanned his surroundings but everything looked the same. Green tents, green trestles, green men.

Not looking where he was going, he slammed into a huge soldier, who shouted at him. Ignoring him, Ben pushed on, past others milling about, lots of people now, all chunnering and laughing. No matter where he looked, he couldn't see any sight of the coffee bar. Frantic, he span around, searching this way and that. Nothing.

With fear gripping him, his eyes wide, gazing out into a sea of unknown faces, he was certain he would cry. And then, a voice broke through his thoughts, calling out to him, "Hey, boy, over here!"

A movement off to his left caught his attention. The flap of a tent entrance closed behind a figure retreating inside. Who was it, Ben wondered; a friend, perhaps that sergeant again? Someone who noticed his predicament and wanted to help? Without another thought, Ben went over and opened the flap.

A soldier sat at a desk with his back towards Ben. "Come in," he said without turning, his voice gruff but non- threatening. "I have something for you."

From inside him, a little voice of warning called to Ben, telling him to stop, turn around and run. But he was torn, torn between his desperation to find Uncle Brendon and go home, and an intense curiosity.

What did this stranger mean, something for him? What kind of something? And who was this man, because by the look of him, even from the rear, he was clearly not the sergeant from before. Swallowing hard, Ben took a step closer.

The man didn't stir. From this close, Ben's eyes scanned across the man's back. This was definitely not the sergeant. This man was leaner, his hair a different colour, and his arms, shirt sleeves rolled up to his biceps, were tanned, the muscles rippling. As Ben leaned forward, the man slowly pushed a piece of paper towards him. Ben noticed the man's hand, dirty, ingrained with grime. Brown too, almost black he was so tanned.

Ben's eyes fell on the paper. No, not a paper. He narrowed his eyes. It was a torn and faded photograph, a man's face staring out at him, grinning openly. A friendly face, a face that Ben thought he recognized. Those features. Could it be...

"*Ben?*"

Ben snatched up the photograph and whirled round, half expecting to see the owner of the voice standing there in the entrance.

"Ben, where the bloody hell are you?"

The voice belonged to his Uncle Brendon, standing just outside the tent entrance, shouting above the noise of the people milling around. Ben sighed and made to go. But then he stopped, thinking that perhaps he should take a moment to ask the soldier what the photograph was, because he was certain he recognized the face. He turned around.

His heart almost stopped. A sudden wave of sickness came over him, his eyes blurring, his legs buckling beneath him. He reached out for a tent post and held on, taking in great gulps of air, trying desperately to steady himself. Breathing hard, he fought against the yawning horribleness of unconsciousness threatening to overwhelm him. Shock. Fear. Disbelief.

He blinked, looking in front of him. There was nothing to see; the desk, the soldier...everything had disappeared.

Chapter Five

The room came back into focus as Henry realized Uncle Ben's voice no longer told his story.

It was the present and they both sat, lost in their thoughts.

A long, drawn out sigh. Uncle Ben pressed his lips together in a grim attempt at a smile. "I need a little break," he said and he leaned forward, gathering up the dirty plates and cups. "These things need washing."

"Does it still exist, that place?" Henry asked as he accompanied his uncle into the kitchen.

Furiously scrubbing the crockery with a faded *Brillo* pad, Uncle Ben shook his head, drying the plates and setting them carefully on the draining board.

He reached out and ruffled Henry's hair. "No," Uncle Ben said, stifling a yawn, "it's long gone." His eyes took on a distant look as he stared back into his lost childhood. "Everything's gone, Henry. All the places where we used to play – the old railway line, Spragg's farm, Darley Dene. All gone, except The Breck. That's still there, although how much it's changed I've no idea as I haven't been there for years."

They went back into the living room. The television remained switched off. Ben couldn't remember the last time he'd spent an evening without watching the television.

"That boy," said Henry quietly, chewing his lips, "The one you hit. Feebles, or something. What happened to him?"

"Peebles?" Uncle Ben seemed to bristle at the mention of the name. "No idea. His parents moved him away after that. God, I could have got into so much trouble over what I did." He shook his head, smiling wryly, "He deserved it, though. I hated him. Still do, probably. Little toad that he was. He must be... I have no idea. Late sixties..."

"There's so much I don't know about you, Uncle Ben."

"Ah, you thought I was some old fuddy-duddy who did a bit of gardening now and then, played bowls up in the park, and drank tea for a hobby."

"No," said Henry, appalled, "not at all. I thought—"

"It's all right," said Uncle Ben, chuckling to himself, "I'm only joking."

"But, you've done things. That Peebles, how could you punch that hard?"

Uncle Ben shrugged, "Don't know. Anger I guess. Mr Taggers, my old P.E. teacher caught wind of it all and one night after school he made me put on some boxing gloves and told me to punch the bag. So I did," he giggled at the memory. "Poor Taggers. His eyes nearly popped out of his head. Said he'd never seen anyone so young who could hit so hard. He set me up with a local boxing club and, well, the rest is history, so they say."

"History? What do you mean?"

"Me. Boxing. Didn't you know?" Henry shook his head. "Nah, probably your Dad conveniently forgot to tell you the details." He shook his head again. "I became a fairly good amateur boxer, Henry. Had a few bouts. Won a few too. By the time I was seventeen I was being groomed to be a professional. When I look back ... Heady times, Henry.

"But what happened?"

Uncle Ben grinned at Henry's wide-eyed enthusiasm. "I was moving some furniture with dear old Eric."

"That's...my Grandpa Eric, isn't it?"

"Yes, you're Dad's dad. Your Dad was very young then. I mean, this must have been...nineteen fifty seven? Eight? Oh, I can't remember. Anyway, your Dad was nothing more than a baby, so Grandpa Eric asked me to help him, seeing as I was probably twice as strong as him. Anyway, this thing – a wardrobe – it was really heavy. We were trying to get it up the stairs when…" He paused as the memory stirred deeply felt emotions within him. He looked away, growing uncertain, his breath coming in short gaps.

"You don't have to go on," said Henry, "not if you don't want to."

"No, no, it's just when I remember it still jars. So stupid it was. I don't know how it happened, but we slipped. The damn thing fell and me, being stupid and thinking I was Superman, tried to stop it. Caught my hand underneath. Crushed." He unconsciously rubbed his right hand as if the pain rekindled, the accident changing his dreams forever. "I broke my hand, almost every finger, severing the nerves. And, from that point on, my boxing days were finished. My left was all right, but no-one's ever made it fighting with just one hand."

"I had no idea, Uncle Ben. I'm sorry."

A slight reddening appeared around Ben's jaw line. He reached out to pull Henry closer and hugged him. "It's all water under the bridge now, Henry. I probably wouldn't have made it to the top anyway."

"Yeah, but you might have done."

Ben stepped away, shrugged. "Unfortunately, life's made up of 'ifs', 'buts' and 'maybes'. Sometimes things happen which are totally beyond our control. Part of growing up is understanding that. No matter how hard we try to do the right thing, something always comes along to thwart our best efforts."

"Is that how it was at this Darley Dene place? You and that rope? It was Neville that cut it, wasn't it?"

Ben gave a slight nod of the head, his eyes narrowing. "Oh yes. It was him all right. You know, I saw him, quite some time ago. Still a big lanky thing, I suppose, but all gnarled up. In a wheelchair. I didn't speak to him. He saw me and gave a little frightened look before pushing himself over to the other side of the street."

"What a toad," declared Henry, echoing his uncle's words that described Peebles.

"Absolutely, Henry. Absolutely."

"You should have punched him as well – I mean, when you were twelve."

Ben thought for a moment, chewing the inside of his cheek, reflective, quiet. When he finally spoke again, his voice grew deeper, darker. "Well, I could have done, but he was a lot bigger than me then. The years have a way of evening everything out. When you're young and someone is two or three years older, that's a lot. But you already know this from the other boys at your school. They seem huge, those ones in Sixth Form, don't they. In about five years, you'll probably be bigger than them." He moved over and switched off the standard light next to the television. "Things sort of evened out with Neville and me, in a funny sort of way. Yes, funny…" His voice trailed away, no explanation coming. His face came up, catching Henry's expectant look, and he quickly added, "I honestly believe people always get their comeuppance…eventually. We should be going to bed."

"But the story, Uncle Ben, it's not finished! I want to know about that soldier, the one who spoke to you, then disappeared."

Ben stared, unblinking. "So you believe that?"

Henry frowned, his lips parting slightly. "You mean it's not real?" He waited, holding his breath.

Uncle Ben's kept his voice very low when he answered, "Oh yes, Henry, it was real all right. It's just that – well, I've never spoken about it to anyone, not since I told my Mum. And that was over fifty years ago. She believed me, every word. How could she not, after what she told me."

The air grew cold and Henry couldn't help but quickly scan the room before turning once more to his uncle. "What did she tell you?"

Ben sighed heavily, "It's late, Henry. Time for bed. I'll tell you tomorrow, after we've been down to the shops. I've got to get some food in, whilst your mum and dad are away."

"But I want to know now, Uncle Ben."

Putting his arm around the young boy's shoulder, Uncle Ben led Henry up the stairs to his bedroom, switching off the lights as he went.

"Tomorrow, Henry. Tomorrow I'll tell you rest of the story of Darley Dene."

Chapter Six

Henry trudged through the supermarket aisles whilst Uncle Ben filled up the shopping trolley with all sorts of goodies. After the checkout, they journeyed home in silence. Unloading cans and boxes into the cupboard, Henry wanted so much to press his uncle about the story, but something in Uncle Ben's demeanour stopped him. Ben appeared distant, the lines drawn deep on his face, so Henry swallowed down his urge to know more.

His thoughts were cut short when the telephone rang. Ben picked up the receiver, listening to the voice on the other end. After a small grunt, he carefully replaced the 'phone on its cradle and turned to Henry.

"What's wrong?" said Henry, unable to ignore the concerned expression on his uncle's face.

"Looks like you might be here for a bit longer," Ben said simply and went over to the television and switched it on. "Things aren't too good, Henry." He looked at his nephew. "Grandpa Frank's no better. I'm sorry."

Without thinking, Henry blurted, "Aren't you?"

"Me? What do you mean?"

"Grandpa Frank. I get the feeling you don't much like him."

"Why do you say that?"

"I don't know. Just a feeling."

"I… it's difficult to explain without me going into all the details. I do like him, of course I do, but we all get ill and we all …" He rubbed his face, clearly struggling to find words which would convey how he felt. "We're not related, you see. Not by blood, I mean." He shrugged. "I suppose I should feel something, but… I'm sorry, Henry, I don't mean to sound so cold. Are you okay?"

Henry nodded, flopping down into the sofa. He nonchalantly picked up the remote control and flicked through the listings. "I'm not sure how I feel about it, to be honest. It's all happened so quickly and I haven't really had much to do with him, so… On the few times I've met him, he did seem like fun. He showed me his train set once. Have you seen his train set?" Uncle Ben shook his head. "It's amazing. It's not just a set, it's a – I think it's called a layout? It's got hills and rivers and there's loads of trains. He let me drive them into an engine shed, a station. It was so cool, but, well, that was ages ago. He used to come to our house, but then his visits just stopped. Nobody said why."

"He's been ill for a long time, Henry. Very ill. Three or four years, I think."

"Wow." Henry looked down at the television remote, idly fingering it, lost in thought. "Uncle Ben, do you ever…" He struggled to find the words. "I don't want to sound personal, or anything, but…"

"Personal? How do you mean?"

"You know, sort of – oh, I don't know, but what's happening to Grandpa Frank, it's got me thinking. Can I ask you something?"

"Of course."

"Are you afraid of dying?"

Ben gave a little laugh, more at his nephew's awkwardness, or so it seemed to Henry, who pushed himself along the sofa as Ben sat down next to him. "What, you think I'm about to drop dead or something?"

"No, it's not that, but you are – well, you know what I mean."

"Yes, I know what you mean – I'm ancient." He chuckled. "I'm sixty five, Ben, not eighty-five. I'm good for a few more years yet, at least I hope I am. They say it's all to do with genes, so I should be okay for a little while. My Mum, your Grandmother, died when she was seventy-six. She died the year you were born."

"Really? I never knew that."

"Didn't your Dad tell you? I thought he would've done."

"No, he didn't say very much. I wish I'd known her. I've only ever seen some old photographs, never heard any stories."

"She had a pretty colourful life. When she was a little girl, she had servants and lived in a fine, big house near the river. It was my Nan who told me all that, as Mum tended not to relive her past, except the little she told me about my Dad. Even then, she forced herself to tell me, to be honest. I doubt if she would have told me anything at all, if I hadn't mentioned what happened when I went up to see the tattoo."

Henry held his breath, hoping this was his chance to press Uncle Ben about the story of Darley Dene. "What was she like?"

"She was a lovely woman. Kind, always singing. God, I remember her singing." He leaned forward, elbows on knees, whimsical, staring at the floor, a slight smile on his face. "She'd be in the kitchen, coming out with all sorts of songs whilst she cooked the dinner. Always cooked the dinner at the weekend, leaving my Nan to rest as she'd done it all through the week. God, it was a funny house back in those days. Hard to believe things have changed so very much."

"And my Dad? He lived with you? You, your mum and your Nan?"

Ben nodded, "Yeah, all together. Mum had met your Dad's dad a few years after the War. It really shook things up when all that happened, I can tell you."

"But your own dad, what do you know about him?"

"I'm not sure of my dad because, as I told you, he died in the War."

Henry sat forward, taking his chance, "Yeah, you said he was a commando. He got killed in Africa. What was he doing in Africa?"

"North Africa. The British were fighting there. Once they'd defeated Rommel at El Alamein, they began to get ready for attacking Europe. My Dad was on a secret mission close to Sicily when he got killed."

"Sicily? Where's that?"

"What do they teach you in school, for crying out loud? It's on the toe of the boot." Henry's face was blank. "Italy? Shaped like a boot? It looks like it's kicked Sicily into the sea?" Ben shook his head in despair as his nephew's face remained a blank. "Never mind." He stood up and made to go.

"Uncle Ben, please – tell me the rest of the story.

You said you would."

"I'm not sure it's for the best, Henry."

"What do you mean, not for the best? You promised."

"I know, but … Look, I couldn't sleep last night, my mind going over all I'd said. The memories, they, well, time plays tricks. That meeting in the tent, I'm not sure it's something I want to talk about. I haven't thought about any of it for over forty years, and back then, I had nightmares. Every damned night." He rubbed his forehead, the anguish changing him. He blew out his cheeks and sat down again. "I still had nightmares up until a few years ago, when I visited a psychic."

"A psychic? What, like a fortune-teller?"

"I was twenty-five, working hard in a departmental store in Liverpool, and there I met Sylvia. After that, my life took a new, uncharted turn, as you might say, due chiefly because of Sylvia's auntie, who was a spiritualist."

"Whoa. That's someone who talks to the dead, isn't it?"

Ben's eyes flashed and for a moment, Henry thought he might have gone too far. But the moment passed and Ben's face relaxed, his eyes moving again to the floor. "On that first meeting, so many years ago, I learned things that I never thought possible. Things that only mum and me knew about. I'd never told Sylvia, or anyone, about what happened, and when this spiritualist … What she told me lightened my burden, so to speak. All my anxieties, fears, overwhelming sense of guilt, it all left me. As did the nightmares." Without warning, he slapped his knees and sprang up, causing Henry to jump, startled. "All right, my little lad, let's get something to eat, then I'll tell you the rest."

Henry rubbed his hands in glee.

Ben smiled.

"I wish we'd spent more time together," said Henry.

"There you go again, thinking I'm going to pop off any time soon."

"I didn't—"

Ben held up his hand. "It's criminal we haven't spent more time with one another, Henry. And, whatever happens, I'm not going to be around forever. So, I think you should come around a lot more, so we can talk and get to know each other.

"I'd love that, Uncle Ben."

"Me too. But, this story, Henry, it's not a pretty one. Things happened that shouldn't have happened, and it took me a long time to come to terms with it. I don't want you thinking badly of me."

"Why would I?"

"Just remember, it was a long time ago. Things were different then – I was different then. After I've told you, you may not want to come here again."

"I can't think why."

"You might, after you know what happened."

"It's a risk I'm willing to take, Uncle Ben. I want you to tell me everything, right to the very end," he smiled, "no matter what."

"All right. Here it is..."

Chapter Seven

"Hi, Trev," said Ben after answering the door to find his friend, who stood there, cold, rock still. Something about the scowl on his face forced Ben to add, "Are you okay?"

Pushing his way into the hallway, Trevor went straight to the kitchen. This was quite usual for Ben's best friend, a frequent visitor to the house, calling round most days. Ben trudged behind him and went to the fridge, pulled it open and poured his friend a drink of juice.

Trevor sipped at it, never taking his eyes off Ben. "Yeah, I suppose I am. I've been thinking about what you told me, about Neville."

"He cut the rope, Trev."

"Well, if you say so..."

"I wouldn't lie about something like that."

"No, okay, but ... Anyway, you don't look so good. What's up?"

"Something happened last night."

"Oh? Is that why you didn't call round? I thought we were going to do something."

"We were, but Uncle Brandon came and took me up to the park, to see the preparations for the tattoo."

"I would have liked that."

"I know, but ... I didn't have time to tell you, but maybe it was good thing you didn't come."

"Oh? Why not?"

"I got lost, and Uncle Brandon, he was crazy. When he found me, he marched me back home and told Mum I'd got lost, that he couldn't find me, had to call the police. Mum screamed at me. I mean *really* screamed, telling me how I was going to force her into a mental home. She sent me straight to bed, without any tea and I lay there in the darkness, listening to the tattoo being played out in the park."

"I heard it too. It sounded great."

"I wanted so much to go, but I ruined everything."

Trevor swallowed down his drink and shrugged. "No harm done," he said philosophically. "Can you come out today?"

"Guess so. Mum's at work. Nan's over at Auntie Kay's. I'll get dressed."

Ten minutes later the two friends were strolling down the road towards Darley Dene. "Who'll be there?" asked Ben, unable to keep the strain from his voice as they inched towards the wall.

Pausing, Trevor gave him a look. "Does it matter, Ben? Look, even if what you said about Nev cutting the rope is true—"

"It *is* true."

"Yeah, okay, but it doesn't matter because you passed the test. You're part of the group now, so just forget about Neville and his stupid antics." He looked around. The occasional car rolled down the road and, across the way at Butler's Garage, a man pushed a brush across the forecourt. He didn't look up. "Come on, before someone sees us." And with that, Trevor hauled himself over the wall and dropped down on the other side. Ben followed.

Almost everyone was there again, gathered around in a tight bunch, laughing. As Ben approached them, Neville looked up, a smirk spreading over his face. The big bully cocked his head to one side, "What you going to do for us today, wimpy? Another circus trick?" Again the chorus of laughter from the others, except Paul and Trevor, standing in silence, as if waiting for something to happen.

Then something did happen.

All his life Ben had tried to do what was right. He'd always been one to 'have a go', liking adventures, being cheeky to the teachers, but he knew the difference between right and wrong. He also knew he had a temper, and Neville's constant goading brought the heat to his face. Something inside snapped. His body grew taut, his lips drawing back over his teeth, his fists bunching. "I'm warning you," he said, struggling to keep his voice under control, "if you don't keep you big, fat mouth shut, I'll –"

"You'll do nothing," it was Paul, stepping forward, pulling Neville back and standing in front of Ben. "Ben, let it go. We're supposed to be friends."

Ben could see Neville's leering face behind Paul's shoulder, the face making him see red. "Then tell him to shut up."

Turning, without hesitation Paul pushed Neville in the chest.

The big teenager teetered backwards, a bewildered look on his face. "What's the matter with you?"

"Just leave him alone, Neville. I'm sick of all this. We came here for the tunnels, to have some fun, not watch you making an idiot of yourself."

"Oh, is that what I'm doing is it?"

"Yes, it is. So, you either pack it in, or you can go home."

For a moment, the air crackled with tension, the two of them standing there like gunfighters about to reach for their guns. Ben waited, hardly daring to breathe. Neville was big for his age, but Paul was older, probably stronger. There was a calmness about him, which was almost menacing.

"Okay," said Neville at last, and he gave a little laugh, "but just know that if he cracks any of those stupid, know-it-all jokes, I'll smack him in the teeth."

Paul nodded, looked back at Ben, who also nodded, and said, "And just so he knows that if he tries, I'll hit him back."

Neville sniggered but Paul seemed satisfied and stepped away.

Breathing hard, Ben sauntered over to Trevor, who stared at his friend wide-eyed. "What were you doing then? He could have killed you!"

Ben shook his head, "I'm just…Trev, I'm sick of it. He thinks because he's big he can do and say what he likes. He's an idiot, and I tell you, if he has another go at me, I'll punch him so hard his teeth will rattle."

"You think you could?"

Ben looked at his friend and his voice, when he spoke, was full of venom, "Oh yes, Trev, I can do it. And do you know what? I'll enjoy it."

It was a small tunnel, dug out from the soft, forgiving earth with the few tools they brought with them. Barely wide enough to accommodate his shoulders, Paul stretched himself out inside, hands behind his head, grinning at a gaping Ben.

"You did this all yourself?"

"All of it. I used spare pieces of timber I found to shore up the roof and it's warm and safe and perfect."

With the doubts circling inside his head, Ben stared at the interior, the walls so smooth, the air so cool. It seemed perfectly safe, nevertheless, he himself would not have felt confident lying inside it, the way Paul did. He would never have trusted those timbers, no matter how solid they might have looked. Paul, however, appeared beefed up with pride at what he had achieved. Beaming from ear to ear, he patted the compacted earth beneath him, "Come on in yourself, Ben – it's warm and dry."

Ben gave a small, embarrassed laugh and shook his head, "I hate confined spaces, Paul." He pulled back from the entrance to the tunnel and stood up, dusting off his knees.

Wriggling his way back outside, Paul joined him. "I used to be like that," he said. "I was stranded on a sandbank you know, up in Morecambe Bay. I was out there with some mates, searching for cockles, and the sea came in at such a rush we got cut off."

"You're joking? What happened?"

"My Dad came and got me. He was none too pleased, I can tell you. Gave me a right rollicking he did. Bit of a hero my dad." Paul looked down at his much younger friend. "Your dad was a bit of a hero too, wasn't he?"

An eerie silence settled over them. Ben looked into Paul's eyes, half expecting to see some glimmer of mockery there. Relieved there was none, Ben titled his head. "What makes you say that?"

Shrugging, Paul said matter-of-factly, "My Mum told me. She's always gassing with your Nan, or your mum. Probably they told her, just in conversation."

"My Nan only told me the other day."

"Oh." Paul shifted his gaze, appearing uneasy, "Sorry, Ben. I thought you knew."

"Mum never tells me anything"

"Probably thinks you're too young. Mums are like that. They think they're sheltering us from the awful truth of something, but it never works. We always end up finding out, and that only makes us feel worse."

Paul's words, spoken with obvious feeling, gave Ben the courage to ask, "Was it like that when your mum and dad broke up?"

Now it was Paul's turn to withdraw into himself, eyes glazing over, lips stretching out into a thin line. For a moment, Ben thought he'd over-stepped the boundaries of friendship, moving into delicate territory, asking questions which really should not have been asked. But then, Paul smiled, the light returning to his eyes. "God, did she ever. She tried everything she could to shield me from the truth. At first, he was going away, then he was staying with my Nan, then he was with a friend who was sick. I just went up to her one day and said, 'Look, what's going on, where's my dad?' So, she told me."

"Weren't you upset? Not having a dad any more, I mean."

Paul frowned. "But I have got a dad, it's just that I don't see him very often." Slowly, the dark look returned, the buoyant mood replaced by something more serious. "But yeah, I was upset at first. Not having him around, not hearing his voice, listening to him whistling in the back garden as he watered the flowers. The house, it seemed *empty*. Not like you though, is it?"

"How do you mean?"

"Your dad. Being..." Paul took a breath, measuring his words.

Before he could continue, however, a great shout erupted from the far end of the rolling wasteland. "What the hell has happened now," Paul muttered and set off towards the commotion, with Ben jogging behind.

The others stood in a loose group, shouting with excitement, huge gaping grins on every face.

Ben followed their frenzied, jabbing fingers and grinned in total disbelief at what he saw.

Chapter Eight

Squeezing through the huddle of boys to get a better look, Ben gazed in astonishment at a single step, half-buried in the earth. Without pausing, Paul went straight to it, sweeping away the soil, little gasping noises escaping from his mouth every few seconds. He turned in triumph. "It's like Howard Carter, and that first step they found on the Tutankhamen dig. Come on, all of you, get the tools and let's find out where this leads."

An explosion of activity followed, with everyone working in a frenzy. Nothing else mattered, all differences set aside, and Ben, aware of Neville beside him, worked as hard as anyone, sweat springing from his forehead, teeth clamped in a grimace, straining every muscle to clear away rock and soil to expose a set of well worn steps, broad and grey in colour. Where they might lead, no one could guess, but they led somewhere. Somewhere that had remained hidden for years.

They stopped about an hour later. The earth, giving way to rubble, proved too compacted to break through. Falling back in the grass, their breath coming in great gulps, they all stared towards the sky. "I wonder what's down there," mused Ben.

"Perhaps it's a grave or something," said one of the boys.

"A grave?" mocked Neville. "It would have to be a bloody great big one, wouldn't it? Nah, those steps don't lead to agrave."

"What then?" asked another.

"Dunno. Secret tunnel maybe."

"Air raid shelter," said Paul. "That's what it'll be, trust me. What do you think, Ben?"

Neville gave his usual scoffing laugh. "Him? What does he know?"

"A lot more than you think," said Paul. then added, "A lot more than you, anyway."

Neville glared, but remained quiet. Ben sensed the dynamics of the group were changing, and not for the better. Paul, whose quiet confidence and impressive knowledge made him the obvious leader, had clashed with Neville several times and Ben saw the effects. Neville seethed just below the surface. If he snapped, could Paul handle him in a stand-up fight, Ben wondered. A showdown was fast drawing close. "Well, Ben?"

Snapping out of his reverie, Ben shrugged. "I think it could be a shelter, yes. Either that, or an underground store." He glanced across the expectant faces turned towards him, hanging on every word. "Whatever it was, it's buried deep, so I'm guessing it might have been hit by a bomb."

"A bomb?" Paul chewed his lip. "From an air-raid?"

"Maybe. But if it is a store, there's a real chance it could hold ammunition."

"What, for guns and that?" cried Neville, his apish grin growing wider.

"Or shells. They might be degraded, which will make them dangerous."

Smirking, Neville looked around for allies to his gloating, "So we're all gonna blow up, is that it wimpy? Is that what you're frightened of, eh?"

Ben's eyes narrowed. "I'm not frightened, I just think we need to be careful."

"Yeah, well you would, wouldn't you – a little Mummy's boy, that's you."

"No I'm not." Growled Ben, voice shaking. He took a step closer to the big bully. "Why can't you just shut up for once?"

Someone groaned, "Here we go again," and Neville, face twisted into a gargoyle mask of sheer rage, rounded towards the others, "Whoever said that had better watch it. We're here to have some good times, not to listen to him moanin' about it being dangerous and stuff. Who cares?"

"I don't know what it is," continued Ben, unconcerned by Neville's outburst, "All I'm saying is we need to be careful."

"Yeah, and you need to stop being such a wimp."

"I'm not a wimp." Ben's fists bunched and Paul stepped up, placing a restraining hand on his arm.

"Yeah, that's right," spat Neville, "let your guardian angel look after you."

Tugging his arm free, it was now Ben's turn to glare, "What is it with you that you've always got to have a go at me? Why am I so special to you, eh, Neville?"

"You're not special to me, you idiot. Why should you be special to me?"

"Well you never stop talking to me. Why don't you just leave me alone?"

"Because you're a wimp, a nance, a mummy's boy, and I hate you."

"I'm none of those things, Neville, do you hear? None of them."

"Oh yeah? Well prove it then."

An expectant hush fell over the group, no one daring to speak or move. Even Paul seemed struck dumb by the exchange.

Taking a deep breath, Ben said, "And how do I do that?" For the first time, his voice broke, and he swallowed hard, doubt creeping into his eyes, coupled with fear. What was he doing, he asked himself. Neville, so much bigger, so much stronger. He'd laugh at the first punch, then quickly smash Ben to the ground, spit in his face, belittle him in front of everyone.

Neville's smile grew wide. "I'll tell you what you can do," he said and reached inside his pocket to pull out a crumpled little carton. He tugged out a cigarette, dangling it in front of Ben's nose. "Smoke it."

Ben stood, like an actor on stage who has forgotten his lines, unblinking, mind a blank, the audience waiting in mounting dread, unsure what might happen next.

His eyes fell on the cigarette. To accept the challenge would only lower himself to Neville's loathsome level. But to decline would hand Neville his victory, and the chants and jeers would echo around the entire bloody world.

"Smoke it?" Ben asked.

"Prove you're not a wimp," snarled Neville.

Ben nodded grimly, reached out and took the proffered smoke, pressing it between his lips as he'd seen actors do in films, and waited. Neville flipped open his lighter and pressed the tiny flame to the end of the cigarette.

Without hesitation, Ben drew the smoke all the way in, deep into his lungs. Almost at once, a great wave of gut-wrenching nausea engulfed him. He battled against it, desperate not to fail, but a series of violent, body shaking coughs overcame him and he bent double, staggering on legs grown suddenly weak, hacking and spluttering, the cigarette dropping to the ground, forgotten. Amidst the roaring laughter of the onlookers, he reeled away like a drunkard and, with his eyes streaming, the embarrassment and shame over-taking the sickness, he broke into a wild, mad run, desperate to escape the gloating, screeching jibes which followed him. A sound which he knew would never leave him.

Without stopping, he got to the wall and scaled it, knees scraping across the coarse stone, hands ripping on the top, hauling himself over to the other side. As he dropped, he stumbled and sat on the pavement, wheezing, lungs and throat on fire. He put his fists into his eyes, rubbing away the tears, trying to rub away the shame.

He failed.

He put his head back and peered towards the sky, knowing his failure would give Neville more than enough ammunition to cause more and more pain, indignation, humiliation. Clenching his fists, he squeezed his eyes shut and roared, "I hate him!"

"Who, sonny?"

Ben gasped and turned, a large ominous shadow falling over him, blocking out the sun. The nausea returned almost at once, but this time it had nothing to do with any cigarette.

The large framed policeman sat astride his bicycle, eying Ben with obvious suspicion. With painful, exaggerated slowness, he dismounted, propped his pedal against the curb, and stepped over to Ben, just as the twelve year old was climbing to his feet.

"And just what do you think you're doing?"

His voice fitted his physique, large and imposing. He waited, a stern look on his florid face.

Ben shrugged, "Nothing. I've just been running, that's all. Out of breath."

The policeman's expression never changed. "Don't lie."

Gaping, Ben realised the man must have seen him coming from over the wall. He tried again. "Honestly. I haven't done anything, *sir.*"

Whether it was the use of the term 'sir', or Ben's obvious distress, but something caused the policeman to appear less stern, his hard jaw relaxing, his eyes losing their glare. "All right, son. Why don't you tell me what you were doing over there?" He nodded towards what lay beyond the wall. "Darley Dene that is. Do you know what that place used to be?"

Ben swallowed hard, torn between wanting to know the secrets, and not wanting to implicate his friends in any way. "I didn't do anything wrong, sir."

"I didn't say you did. I just want to know what you've been doing over there. The truth, sonny."

"Just looking around, sir. There's not a lot to see, so I came away."

The policeman took a loud sniff. "Been smoking?"

Well – yes, sir, I have. Sorry. I tried one, but *only* one. I didn't like it, so I threw it away."

"Threw it away? Hope you haven't started a fire."

"I shouldn't think so… sir."

"Well, if that's all you've been doing…"

"It is, sir. Honestly."

"And who is this person you hate so much, eh?"

The sound of Ben's heart banging against the wall of his chest surely could be heard by everyone, not just the policeman. He forced a tiny snigger. "Oh, just some mates of mine. Trying to show off."

"So there's more of you in there, is there?"

"What, now? No, no, they've all gone – I mean, *we've* all …" His voice trailed away. "We didn't do anything wrong. I promise."

"All right then." The policeman went to turn towards his bicycle but stopped. "So, not on your own, and up to no mischief. Is that what you're telling me?"

Ben shook his head before blurting out, "Yes – I mean…Oh God…sorry."

Releasing a long sigh, the policeman moved past Ben and stood on his tiptoes to peer over the wall. Ben took his chance and went to creep away.

"I don't want to catch you here again," snapped the policeman, pulling up Ben sharply. "You understand? This place is dangerous."

Curiosity fired, Ben frowned. "Dangerous? Why is it dangerous, sir?"

"Never you mind. You just do as I tell you. You understand?"

"Yes sir."

"Good. Now, clear off before I take your name and address."

Not needing any further prompts, Ben jogged across the road, taking one last glance backward to see the policeman swinging his leg over the wall. Fighting down the rising panic, Ben broke into a run and didn't stop until he was back home.

Chapter Nine

Later that same afternoon, as Ben poured out a cup of tea for his Nan, there came a persistent pounding on the front door. "If that's the insurance man, the money's on the side," called Nan from her room, but it wasn't the insurance man, it was Trevor. And he looked worried.

Ben stood aside as Trevor came in, out of breath and flustered. Before Ben could even open his mouth, Trevor regaled what had happened. "After you ran off, a busy came to our camp."

"A busy?"

"Policeman, copper."

"Oh God. What did he want?"

"You didn't see him?"

"No. Not … What happened?"

Trevor blew out a loud breath and walked into the kitchen. Without asking, he took down a cup from their rack and filled it up with water from the tap. He drank it down, gasping when he finished. "He'd come over the wall and caught us all smoking and larking about. One or two ran, but Neville and Paul braved it out. Paul tried to tell him some story, but Neville, he started strutting about, saying it was all your fault."

"All *my* fault?" Ben slumped into a chair and stared. "Oh God…"

"Paul laid into him."

"What, they had a fight?"

"Oh yeah," said Trevor, his voice leaden with meaning, "You should have seen it, Ben. It was – God, it was great. They started off pushing each other, then Neville punched Paul. I mean *really* punched him. Even the copper was surprised. Paul went down, but he came up again and hit Neville back, once, twice, three times. Every punch was hard enough to take someone's head off, but not Nev's. He just sort of hunched himself up and got Paul in some sort of wrestling hold. Anyway, they fell down, and Nev got on top, pinned him. I think he was going to beat him, Ben. That's when the policeman had had enough and grabbed him. Well, more than that, he lifted him off his feet – God, that copper was huge. Anyway, then he tells us that we're stupid, that there's all sorts of underground passages in the ground, maybe even – get this – unexploded bombs! He said he'd be looking in again, and if he caught us, he'd take us to the station."

Before he realized it, Ben said, "Oh God, Trev, he got me as I came over the wall. He just came out of nowhere."

A stony silence followed. Ben felt the blood drain from every fibre of his body. Trevor's look was terrible. "You just said you didn't see no copper."

"I... I didn't see him, as such, but when I—"

"Did you tell him we was in there? Did yeh?"

"Of course not. God, Trev, why would I do that?"

"I dunno, but you just said ... Anyways, I don't think you did, and neither does Paul, but Neville, he was really angry, Ben. I've never seen him like that before. He shouted it was you, that he was going to kick your teeth in."

Ben put his face in his hands. "Oh God..."

"The copper, he takes them both home, to stop another fight. I went round to see if Nev was okay, and his mum tells me to get lost. As if it was *my* fault. Nev comes out of the front room, right, and his face...I know he got hit by Paul, but his mum must have hit him too, after the copper took him home. Poor Nev, he got a right beating he did. And when his dad gets home, he'll get another one. His dad is really hard. I don't think we'll be seeing him for a while anyway."

Ben sat in silence whilst Trevor opened up the biscuit barrel and helped himself to a few custard creams. He munched them down with gusto, then, with mouth still full, he reached into the cupboard under the sink and brought out a bottle of lemonade. Ben simply stared at the kitchen tabletop, images of policemen, tunnels and fights flitting through his mind. It was all such a mess, and now Neville hated him even more and would take the first opportunity to beat him to a pulp. Life was becoming a nightmare.

He looked up to see Trevor finishing off his drink, smacking his lips, saying, "There's something more."

"I can't listen," snapped Ben, shoving back his chair so violently it toppled over and fell to the floor with a crash. His Nan called from her room, "Is everyone all right in there?"

"Yes, Nan," shouted back Ben, his breath coming in short gulps, "it's all right."

"Nothing broken I hope."

"No, Nan." Ben leaned forward across the kitchen table, his voice little more than a whisper, "If you're going to tell me that Neville has promised to kick my head in, you've already said it, so—"

"No, nothing like that. It's Paul, he said you had to do something else."

"Something else? What do you mean, 'something else'?"

Trevor smiled, putting his mug gently down on the table-top. "He says that the only way you can get everyone back on your side is to do another test."

"What? You've got to be joking."

Shaking his head, Trevor couldn't help but smile. "This is classic, this is. He said we had to go down to the shunting-yard. You and me."

"The shunting-yard? Oh God, I hate it down there..."

"Yeah, thought you'd be pleased."

"I had nightmares the last time. Trev, what sort of test does he want me to do?"

"I'll tell you all about it on the way."

"But, why you as well? It's me who—"

"I'm your friend, Ben. And right now, I'm the only one you've got."

Chapter Ten

The almost preternatural sound of groaning cogwheels, pistons and steam screamed shrilly into Ben's ears, set his teeth on edge and caused him to hunch up. Grimacing, he followed Trevor skipping over the railway tracks which led towards the long, snaking train of carriages, waiting like ranks of prehistoric beasts, grim, huge and frightening.

They cut across Darley Dene to an old duckboard path and the vast area set aside for the distributing, organizing and rearranging of rail bound freight. The marshalling, or shunting yard. And now, so close to the silent, waiting trucks, their locomotives at their head, Ben's chest tightened, as it always did when he thought of trains. He'd had a recurring nightmare for a long time now, of being trapped between several railway tracks, not knowing which were gaps or which were pairs of parallel rails. As he stumbled, hesitating, not knowing which way to go, from out of the night, a huge steam locomotive came hurtling towards him, the blast from its funnel freezing him like a rabbit caught in the headlights. Which way to go, left or right, or to stay where he was? As he leaped from one side to the other, each move seemed to place him directly in the path of the oncoming engine. Then it was too late, no more decisions to make, right or wrong, for the thing was upon him, and the impact was massive and total...and he'd sit bolt upright in his bed, heart beat thumping, the sweat springing across his brow, wanting to cry out, but knowing he was too old for that now.

The horror of it was almost too much to bear, and he'd slump back down amongst his blankets and lie there, looking at his wall, trying to regain his senses until he would drift off.

But this, this was no dream. This was real, and the sheer size of the freight trucks filled him with dread. Why had they come here, what kind of initiation test was this? He turned on Trevor, trying to disguise his fear with false anger. "What is this all about, Trev? We're here now, so tell me what this test is."

Trevor gave a little chuckle as he wandered over to one of the trucks. He absently flicked a piece of rectangular card, no bigger than an envelope, protruding from a metal holder on the side of the truck. "See these," he said, "on each card is detailed the cargo aboard, where it was loaded, and where it's going. The guards, or whatever they're called, use them to sort all this lot out."

Overawed, Ben peered up and down the long, long row of trucks. To the left, to the right, two great lines, featureless and uniform. If the cards were lost, or removed, the only way to check on what each carried would be to open them up and look inside, a task a small army would take days to complete. Ben caught Trevor's look. He gaped. "You mean...?"

Trevor nodded, casually pulling out the card from the side of the nearest truck. "That's right, Ben. You've got to snatch as many of these as you can and take them back to Paul. Then you'll be a full member and Neville can go and jump."

Ben scanned the line of trucks again. He was no angel, had found himself in a few scrapes, but this, this was something completely different. This was malicious, a premeditated act – a court appearance and a sound thrashing would follow if the guard caught him. Images of his Mum's drawn, despairing face, tear-stained, gazing at him with unbelieving eyes, 'Why are you doing this to me, Ben? Do you want to put me into a mental hospital?' That was Mum's usual cry, but this time, it could be real. This could send Mum over the edge, something Ben did not want to do.

Conscious laden, Ben stepped away, shaking his head. "No, Trev, I can't do this. I want to go home now." Try as he might, he could not keep the wailing note from his voice. Trevor, smile frozen on his face, tensed and stepped up to his friend, his features becoming hard. It was a look of menace. His eyes narrowed, jaw jutting forward. "You've got to, Ben. If you don't, Neville will kick your teeth in, and Paul won't help."

Trapped, torn between conscience and the desire to belong, Ben focused in one the slips of card. They dominated his vision, impossibly huge, forcing him, calling him, begging him to reach out and pluck them from their holsters one by one. Building up from deep within him, uncertainty, confusion and despair battled for supremacy. He no longer knew what to do. Swirling images of his Mum, Neville, Paul, the policeman, jeering, laughing faces, mouths open, mocking him. And amongst them, sadly shaking her head, stood Nan.

Without knowing why, he shot out his hand and grabbed the nearest card, yanking it away from the truck so violently it ripped. Then he was running along the great train, pulling out cards as he went, sometimes tearing them, sometimes missing them altogether, but never stopping.

Glancing behind him, he saw Trevor doing the same, but with greater care. Already his collection appeared twice that of Ben's.

Confused and anxious, Ben stopped, sucking in the air. He'd run hard, outpacing Trevor by an appreciable margin. But when he looked down at his fist, his collection of cards seemed meager by comparison. Deciding to back track, he took a step to begin retrieving those cards he's missed, and pulled up, rock solid, opening his mouth to shout out a warning. But already it was too late.

From nowhere, a black-clad man materialized from between the trucks. Like some horrifying, gothic bird of prey, his great hands reached out like talons, catching Trevor around the throat in one fluid movement. Ben watched, transfixed with shock at the suddenness of it all. The man, wild with anger, face contorted into a mask of rage, saliva drooling from his clenched teeth, set about cuffing Trevor around the head.

Ben stood as if in a daze, an onlooker to the scene played out before him, Trevor screaming, "I'm sorry, I'm sorry," over and over again. But the man wouldn't stop. He kept hitting Trevor, back-handed slaps across the face, gripping him in his other hand, holding him limp and bloody. Trevor, his voice reaching new heights of terror, sagged in the man's grip, legs buckling under him, the cards slipping from numbed, senseless fingers to fall, like autumn leaves, to the ground, the wind catching them and whipping them up into the air.

Spotting this, the man ceased the beating and released Trevor, who dropped to his knees, blubbering, blood trailing from split lips and nostrils. Desperate, the man floundered around, trying to gather up the cards before the wind scattered them further still.

Ben watched, unable to move, his body quivering, strength all gone. A thought came into his mind, awful in its probability – there would be more men, more guards, perhaps police, cutting off all exit routes. He caught Trevor's battered face and saw the glimmer of consciousness.

"Come on," screamed Ben, throwing down his own collection of cards, "Come on, Trevor, get up and run for it."

The sound of Ben's snapped the man out of his efforts to save the cards. He made a wild grab for Trevor, who proved too quick, too nimble. Throwing himself to the side, Trevor somersaulted over the dirt to his feet. Dodging around the man, Trevor broke into a sprint.

With Ben setting the pace, the two youngsters outpaced the man in black with ease and soon he was nothing but a speck, his arms waving wildly in the air, his voice indistinct but full of rage.

All they had to do was keep running and find a way out.

The growing sound of steam hissing from between the great drive wheels of the locomotives told them they were drawing close to the front of the trains. Not a fact which brought them any sense of relief. They were trespassers, vandals, criminals. Once caught, the police would arrest them. Court, fines, juvenile detention centres.

Groaning as the awful pictures whirled around in his head, Ben ground to a halt and grabbed his friend's arm. "We have to find another way."

"But where?"

Turning his back on the array of engines, Ben pointed across to his left. "Come on, this way," and he darted between the trucks, nimbly stepping over the couplings, to cross another line and repeat the procedure. At this juncture, there seemed more trucks than before. They certainly appeared closer, taller, and every time he moved between them, the chain links clattered, as if the wagons were waiting, waiting for the chance to squeeze together and trap him. Dismissing this as fancy, Ben pushed on, and when there was only one set of trucks ahead, he turned in triumph, ready to cry out to Trevor, to let him know they were free.

His heart almost stopped.

Trevor had gone.

There was no sign of him, only the featureless lines of trucks to see and the steady pant of steam engines to hear.

He scanned along the spread of wagons, got down on his knees and gasped. Trevor lay sprawled in the dirt. He must have tripped and somehow become caught between a set of couplings.

Ben broke into a run. As he approached, he heard Trevor crying, and he could see why. A massive gash ran up the length of his shin, cutting deep and exposing the white of his bone. The blood wasn't running fast yet, but the pain must have been colossal, because Trevor never cried, and now he was yelping like a baby.

"Oh God, Ben. Get me out, get me out."

Ben looked at his friend. Trevor was trembling, the terror etched into every line of his face, tears cutting through the grime, his leg useless beneath him. He had slipped into the space between the coupling and Ben, to the side, strained to reach over, get his hands under his friend's armpits, and attempt to haul him up.

The angle was too acute and Ben could not bring his strength to bear. He stepped back, blowing out his breath. "I can't do it," he said.

"You have to, Ben. Please. I can't move. My leg … Ben, *please.*"

There was no choice. He would have to try again. He looked around, certain black-uniformed guards would be swarming towards him, but there was nothing. He turned, to renew his efforts.

And then the trucks began to move.

A great, awful grind of metal against metal filled the air and through wild, terrified eyes, Ben realized what was happening. The whole train moved, each and every truck, an enormous yank back and then a sudden lurch forward, as if some invisible hand of enormous power was pulling them. But it was no hand, it was the locomotive, massive and unstoppable, far down at the front, starting its job of shunting the trucks towards another siding.

Trevor was screaming, not with pain this time, but blind panic and Ben saw why; Trevor's trouser leg had somehow become caught amongst the chains of the coupling. Soon, the forward motion of the train would drag him relentlessly forward, or crush him beneath the wheels.

Desperate now, Ben gripped his friend's arm but despite pulling with all his might, he made no headway. He gritted his teeth and with one last, desperate tug, he felt the material of his friend's trousers ripping. There might be a chance, but he wasn't completely free yet. Ben got his hands under his friend again, but fear turned him into a helpless mass, sobs overwhelming him, body a dead weight.

Without warning, the trucks stopped. Having travelled no more than nine inches, they now grew were still.

Trevor's face came up, the relief palpable, and then he fainted. Ben strained, Trevor's body impossibly heavy, and, as he heaved, he lost his footing and stumbled backwards, flopping down in the dirt with a grunt, more out of despair than from pain. He didn't pause. With teeth clamped together, he set to it again, but the material of Trevor's trousers was all chewed up amongst the coupling. There was no way to free his friend without taking those damned trousers off.

And then he heard it. A voice, at once calm, assured and friendly. "Let me help."

The notion of being frightened to death never usually entered Ben's thoughts, but he very nearly did die at that moment, such was the intense shock he experienced when a man, slim and brown haired, appeared as if from nowhere. He reached over and gently pulled Ben away. Ben watched, unable to think or believe what he was seeing, as the man produced a penknife and sliced through the piece of caught trouser material, then lifted Trevor free with ease. He laid him down on the ground just as the train gave another, sickening lurch, and began to slowly and relentlessly move forward.

"You were lucky, or should I say he was." The man looked into Ben's face and Ben gasped.

His mouth fell open, disbelief gripping him, turning his stomach to water and he fell down onto his backside, and gazed in horror at the man. The man who had saved Trevor. He knew that man.

He was the soldier from the military tattoo, the one who gave him the photograph. The one who had disappeared.

Chapter Eleven

If it was a dream, Ben couldn't be sure. He'd passed out, almost as soon as the man spoke to him. And now, blinking into the white sky, of that man, there was no sign. He sat up, and all he saw were the wagons and Trevor, lying on the ground. Pulling himself up, he gave his friend a sharp push with his foot. Trevor stirred, then yelped, clutching at his shin, the pain creasing through his features. Releasing a rasping sigh of agony, eyes squeezed shut, he surrendered to Ben's gentle arms, helping him to his feet. He looked at his friend, a single tear rolling down his cheek, "Ben, God Almighty, you saved me."

Ignoring him, Ben laced his arm around his friend's waist and, together, they hobbled away from the shunting yard, struggling across the marshes, every inch feeling like a mile, every step sending shooting pains through them both

Sobbing incessantly, Trevor's eyes rolled as he slipped into his own private world of agony. Ben, aware of how much each step took out of his friend, did the best he could, urging him on, telling him all would be all right in the end, when they got home, when they sat down and relaxed and drank cream soda from a green bottle. How much the ordinary seemed so very special.

Knowing the marsh proved forever hazardous, even in the best of times, Ben measured each step with great care. The duckboards, laid down to make going a little easier, were way down to his left. Too far. If he crossed to them, he might stumble, perhaps even sink into the treacherous, shifting clumps of undergrowth. And if the guards came, there would be no chance to run. They would block off the escape route, trapping them both with no chance of escape.

Stopping, with his right arm supporting his friend, he cast his eyes about the marshland, desperate to find a pathway, some hope of a way home. So many bottomless pools claimed unwary travellers, often drunks crossing the marsh from Bidston, capturing them amongst the dense weeds, dragging them down where they drowned.

Knowing how desperate the situation now was, Ben's breathing grew ragged, the fear gnawing away, knuckled fists of terror kneading around inside his guts. He faced a simple choice – stagger on and almost certainly fail, or leave Trevor here, run home to get help.

He squeezed his eyes shut. Help meant the police. Questions, demands, accusations, incessant, never ending until he revealed the truth. It was just too terrible to contemplate.

But there was no choice. He dragged in a deep breath. Somehow, he had to cross the more, and take Trevor home. He'd conjure some fanciful tale, of how they were playing, his friend slipped and fell down a cliff face, caught his shin and …

From out of the distance, a figure appeared, striding towards them, either deliverer or avenger. A guard, a policeman, Ben did not know. Nor did he care. Despair overcoming him, he could run no more. But he could not leave his friend either. So he gently lowered Trevor to the ground, knelt down beside him, and waited.

As the figure drew closer, Ben realized who it was. The soldier, from the tattoo. So none of it was a dream. Here he was, not a figment of his imagination, or a shadowy figure in the gloom, but a living, physical being.

The soldier stopped within a stride of the two boys, his face a featureless map. "Follow me," he said, his voice calm and assured. "Tread where I tread." Then he turned and set off across the sodden, entangled and treacherous marshland. Pausing only to gather his courage, Ben lifted Trevor up and moved after the figure of the mysterious soldier.

Within a few steps, Ben realized how far they still needed to go before the marsh gave way to firmer ground. He wanted to shout out to the soldier, who marched ahead with all the confidence of someone who knew the area well, but he was too far away. Trevor, so heavy in Ben's arms, lolled and moaned. Another half dozen steps, arms screaming with the effort, muscles burning, sweat dripping into his eyes, Ben stopped.

He wanted to go on. He knew he must. But the next step proved too much and his strength left him in a rush and he slumped to the ground, Trevor protesting with loud, a pain- filled groan.

Ben sat, rubbing his forearm and bicep, watching the soldier disappearing into the distance. Perhaps he should have called out to him, but something other than the distance prevented him. Something stirred inside, a simmering unease. A feeling that perhaps a strange, unspoken danger resided within the soldier, that this saviour was more than he seemed.

"What in the name of everything that is holy are you doing here?"

Snapping his head around, Ben made to get up, the apology already forming on his lips. He didn't wish to appear ungrateful, the soldier's help almost certainly saving them from either capture or perhaps even death.

As Ben went to speak, he saw that the man standing before him was not the soldier, but a stranger, big and burly, swathed in a huge, flapping raincoat. Gasping, Ben again tried to stand.

"Careful, laddie," the stranger said, holding up his hand, "this marsh is deadly." He stooped down to examine Trevor, sprawled out on his back, mumbling something incoherent. "Good God, this boy has a fever." He placed a large hand on Trevor's forehead and looked up at Ben. "What the merry hell have you been doing?"

"Nothing," Ben blurted out automatically, his mind reeling.

"Well, it's obvious you've been doin' something. Look at his bloody leg. We need to get him to hospital."

Scooping Trevor up in his great arms as if he were no heavier than a toy doll, he scowled at Ben. "You follow me. I'll take you to the top of the hill even though you probably know the way. You certainly seem to have made it easily enough so far." He set off, Ben sheepishly following, giving no explanation to the man about the soldier guiding the boys across the marsh.

With every step, he looked around, trying to catch a glimpse of the soldier and offer his thanks. But, having disappeared once more into the shadows, there was no sign of him.

Before long, the ground under foot grew more solid and soon they were tramping across Darley Dene. Sinking beyond the horizon, the early evening Sun cast the whole area in a strange, eerie orange hue. Ben caught sight of the tunnel Paul made, the steps they'd discovered and, further off in the distance, the rope swing. But, bathed in that eerie glow, everything seemed unreal, mere shadows, the smattering of memories, so very distant. Alien.

And there, by the unearthed steps, hazy grey and indistinct in the weakening sunlight, the figure of the soldier.

Ben stopped and blinked, narrowed his eyes, focusing hard.

The soldier's arm came up. Then he turned and descended those steps to disappear into the very ground itself.

Chapter Twelve

"Come on, laddie, it'll be dark soon."

Ben tore himself away from the disappearing soldier's image and gawped towards the stranger. Numb with exhaustion, his mind confused and in disarray, the light played tricks with his senses. That had to be the answer. To prove it, he looked again. Nothing, the few unearthed steps silent and alone. Relieved, albeit unease continuing to cling to his neck muscles, he set off once more.

Emerging at last through overgrown bushes, Ben stepped out into the road. It was an exit he did not know even existed.

"Been coming this way for years," said the stranger, carefully laying Trevor down. "I'm going to find a 'phone box and ring for an ambulance. You wait here and make sure your friend is all right."

Ben nodded but, surrendering to the sudden rush of emotions bombarding him, all he could manage was a feeble grunt in reply. He watched the stranger crossing the road towards St. Luke's church, and slumped down beside his friend.

Regaining full consciousness, Trevor sat up, letting out a prolonged hiss as he tried to flex his leg. He winced, but continued to straighten out his limb. Already a scab was forming over the wound, but the surrounding flesh was raised and angry. "Mum's going to kill me," he muttered.

"You?" Ben pressed his fingers into his eyes, "I'll never be allowed out again after this."

They both sat on the pavement, the worries of the entire world pressing down on them. Neither spoke for a long time as they gazed into the road.

"Look," said Trevor at last, "I have an idea."

"I can't be doing with any more of your ideas," said Ben with feeling.

"Just listen." Trevor's voice had regained some of its former resolve. "Whatever happens, we can't tell anyone what we did. If we do, the police will throw the book at us." He reached forward and gently massaged his leg, straining not to touch the actual wound. "God, this hurts like anything. I slipped as I stepped over the chains and the damned thing scraped right through me."

"I know, Trevor, I was there – remember?"

"Yeah, of course I do," Trevor gave his friend a meaningful look, "and I won't ever forget what you did Ben. Not ever."

"Well…I didn't actually do very much, to be honest."

"Only saved my life, you idiot."

Ben looked away, anxious not to reveal the truth. "You would have done the same."

"Yeah, maybe so, but …" He clamped his hand on his friend's shoulder. "I'm sorry for getting you into all of this. It was stupid."

Ben shrugged, still not able to meet Trevor's eyes.

"I'm going home," said Trevor with a sigh, hauling himself to his feet. "I know a short cut, over the back of Butler's garage."

Leaping to his feet, Ben gripped Trevor's sleeve. "What, are you crazy? Trev, that bloke's gone to get an ambulance. He says you need to stay here and not move."

"I know what he said, Ben, but I ain't hanging around here for an ambulance. There'll be too much explaining to do."

"Yeah, but your leg."

"It's much better now, promise."

"It isn't. Bloody hell, look at it."

And they did, the both of them. A sliver of white bone protruded from beneath the scab. No bigger than a matchstick, Ben's had the almost irresistible urge to reach out and touch it.

"I'll be all right. Look, you have to get your story straight. We got lost on the marsh, yeah? I fell, cut me leg on a hidden tree or something. Okay? No mention of trains or anything like that. In fact, we never even went down there – we stayed playing in Darley Dene."

Ben shrugged, eyes still glued on the shard of bone.

"Okay?" Trevor shook him, voice adopting a raw edge, impatient, close to anger.

Ben nodded, his face coming up to meet his friend's glare. "Okay."

"Good," continued Trevor. "I'm feeling fine now, I really am." As if to prove it, he put his weight down onto his stricken limb. At once, the colour drained from his face and he swayed slightly, biting down the pain. "Fuck that hurts."

"Trev, you have to—"

"No, I'm okay. Honest. I'm off and you tell that bloke our story, okay? But, whatever you do, don't tell him where I live. I'll call round tomorrow." And with that he was gone, limping as he went, crossing the road and then bearing left, over the brow towards Butler's garage and the secret way to his house that only he knew. For a long time, Ben just looked, his body numb.

It might have been a quarter of an hour later when the stranger reappeared, his face flushed. "Damned thing," he snapped as he stepped up onto the pavement, "it wouldn't connect. Out of order I think. I went down the slip to the other phone box but it was – hey, where the bloody hell is your mate?"

"He said he was feeling better, so he went home."

"He did *what*? If that legs gets infected, he'll—"

"He'll be fine. His mum's a nurse."

"Is she, by God."

Ben stood resolute. Another lie to add to the catalogue.

They set off along Mill Lane, Ben silent, running through the story he needed to tell his mum in order to save himself from a battering. His mind was also full of questions. Where had the soldier appeared from, and how did he know Ben and Trevor were there, in the marshalling yard? Of course, Ben was grateful. Without the soldier's intervention, who knows what might have happened. He shuddered when he imagined the train moving, crushing Trevor under its wheels.

No, it wasn't that the man had helped them, it was the sheer incredibility of it all. Why was the soldier there and, more mysteriously, where had he disappeared to?

With his thoughts preoccupied, Ben did not notice the stranger had stopped. "What's the matter?"

"I think it would be a good idea if you told me where you lived."

Smiling, Ben pointed to the blue gate not six feet away. "Right here."

The man gave a little start. Frowning deeply, he went up to the door and pressed the doorbell. Ben waited sheepishly, but before long the door eased open and there stood Mum, her eyes so wide Ben thought they would pop out.

"Oh Ben," she said, rushing forward to grab him in a tight embrace, kissing his cheeks repeatedly, "Where have you been? I've been worried sick."

The stranger gave a little cough, "I found him down at Darley Dene."

Mum's eyes flashed. "Oh no, not again."

"It's all right – I mean, *he's* all right. I reckon he must have got lost or something. He was crossing the marsh..."

"The marsh?" Mum looked at Ben again, gripping his shoulders, the first signs of anger coming into her face, "What were you doing there, Ben? Haven't I told you never to go across the marshes?"

"He knew his way," the stranger said quickly, before Ben could offer up his own explanation. "I was watching him and his friend. They didn't put a foot wrong. He must know one of the old pathways."

It was now Ben's turn to frown. If he'd been watching, hadn't the stranger seen the soldier, the one responsible for guiding the boys across the treacherous undergrowth?

The stranger continued, "His friend hurt his leg quite badly. I meant to 'phone for an ambulance but the blasted telephone box wasn't working. By the time
I got back, the other fella had scarpered."

"Trevor was it?" Mum gave Ben a knowing look. "Was he badly hurt, Ben?"

"He'd fallen and cut his leg on a branch. Really hurt himself he did. But I think he'll be all right."

"Well, I can't thank you enough." Mum pulled back from Ben, ruffling his hair, "He's going to be the death of me one of these days. Go on in and get yourself washed. Nan's got your tea in the oven."

Before disappearing into the house, Ben paused and looked at the man, giving him a smile and a nod of appreciation. In return, the man winked.

Ben slipped into the front room and stood behind the door, listening to the conversation on the front step.

"He's very precious to me," said Mum. "The man of the house, if you know what I mean."

"I think I do." A little laugh, then a long sigh. "I'd best be off. You couldn't tell me if there was a pub around here, could you? I'm spitting feathers."

"Yes, there's two – at the bottom, there's the Poole Inn, and at the very top, The Tower."

"Ah, well, as I'm going that way, I'll walk up to the top."

"You can't miss it. I can offer you a cup of tea, or something, before you go? I mean, I'm so very grateful."

"Another time, perhaps. I really should be getting home."

"Ah, yes. Your wife will be expecting you."

"No, no, nothing like that. I have no wife, only my dog. I've left him indoors. He gets somewhat destructful to say the least if he's left alone too long." He paused. "Is there such as word as 'destructful'?"

She laughed, "Goodness, I don't know. Sounds like there should be."

"Yes. Yes, it does doesn't it?" He laughed again, joining her in that brief moment of merriment. For some moments, there were no words. "Well, whatever," continued the stranger, voice sounding a little awkward, "he destroys everything in sight."

"Well, thank you again. If you hadn't been passing goodness knows what would have happened crossing that damned marsh."

"I was off down to visit a friend of mine on Breck Road when I happened to see the boys. I live in the Village you see, and I usually just walk all the way along, but ... Well, it's hard to explain, but I took a detour and cut across Spragg's Farm. Not sure why, because it was out the way... Curious..."

"Well, what a good job you did. I can't imagine what would have happened if you hadn't found the boys."

"Yes, but, saying that, I'm sure they would have been all right, knowing their way across the marsh like that. They seem very resourceful."

"I've told and told Ben to stay away, not only from the marsh, but also Darley Dene."

"It's a dangerous place. I've heard rumours they might be digging it all over, to make way for an approach road to a proposed tunnel under the Mersey."

"Really? Well, that will certainly make me rest easier."

"They crossed the marshland like proper experts. They seemed to know every step to take. Clever."

"I'd say just plain naughty."

"Yes, well, anyway..."

Ben heard the stranger's feet shuffling, as if he were making ready to go. Then he stopped. "Look, this might be totally inappropriate, but...well...what I mean is...that cup of tea...Perhaps we could, I mean, perhaps I could, buy you a cup of tea. At the 'Mario Coffee Shop', say...one evening this week? That's if you're not, you know...not..."

She laughed at his awkwardness. "I'd love to. Tuesday. I'll be there just after six."

Taking this as his cue, Ben slipped out from behind the door and crept into the kitchen, making as if he had been there for some time, reaching into the oven to pull out his tea. He heard the front door closing and, from the hallway came Nan's voice, sharp, demanding.

"Who was that man?"

"I've no idea," said Ben's mum, "Never seen him before."

"Well, you seemed to be very pally with him."

"Where you listening?"

"I might have been. Made a date did you?"

"What if I did? It's not a crime, is it?"

"No... but you need to be careful, Mary. That's all I'm saying."

"Oh for God's sake, Mum. He's obviously a descent sort – look how he brought Ben home the way he did."

"Yes, well, you never know."

"Ah, that's just silly. Anyway, he's the first man to ask me out for years."

Ben almost choked on his meal's first mouthful. He stopped as both his mum and grandmother came into the kitchen.

"Are you going?"

"I might be."

Ben peered at her over a fork piled up with mince and potato. "Mum, for God's sake, you can't."

His mum glared. "You as well? What's the matter with you lot? Aren't I allowed to have a bit of fun?"

"Of course you are," snapped Nan, going over to the sink to dry some dishes, "It's just that I'm concerned. Worried. You've been hurt too many times, and I don't want—"

"It's a date – not a marriage proposal. And anyway, it's only a cup of tea or coffee at Mario's. I haven't been there for... God, for years. All I do is work every day of the week, including Saturdays, trying to keep this roof over our heads... I just think I deserve a bit of fun, that's all. There's no harm in it for crying out loud." And with that she flounced out, the start of a tear appearing in the corner of her eye.

Nan watched her go, shaking her head sadly. "I hope she's not going to get hurt again," she said to herself, forgetting about Ben, who still sat there, watching her keenly. But although he didn't speak, his imagination was already working overtime, most of the images in his head not to do with his Mum and the stranger, but the appearance of the mysterious soldier. He may have hallucinated him disappearing underground, but the way he helped Trevor was no hallucination. It was real. So the question remained – who was he?

Chapter Thirteen

Set in stone, like a line of statues, the boys stood in silence and watched his approach. Breathing steadily, moving his eyes from one to the other, Ben tried to keep himself loose but he knew that this meeting was going to be difficult. He stopped and gave a little nod to Paul before looking Neville squarely in the eyes. For a few painful moments, the tension rose, fizzing through the air like an electric charge. Ben let it go, averting his eyes, and returning them to Paul.

"We saw Trev," Paul said in an even voice. "His leg is pretty bad, Ben."

"How did he do it?"

Ben turned unblinking towards Neville. "Didn't he tell you?"

Neville ignored the barb, smiled and calmly replied, "Why don't *you* tell us?"

"He fell. In the marsh. He caught his leg on a half buried tree branch."

"That's a lie."

Without warning, Paul came forward and clamped his hand on Ben's shoulder. "Why don't you tell us how it really happened – and where you had you been?"

Ben, aware of the dare instigated by Paul, knew it was pointless in not revealing everything, so he went straight into a dramatic explanation, making out as if Trevor was the main player, making no mention of how Ben almost certainly saved his friend's life by dragging him out from between the couplings. And he daren't tell them of the soldier. Who would believe it? After all, he hardly believed it himself.

As the story came to its close, Paul gave a laugh, "You surprised us all right with what you did, taking those cards." He put his arms around the much shorter boy and hugged him, "You're in, mate. What you and Trev did, going down there into the marshalling yard, it was spectacular." He pulled away, leaving his hands on Ben's shoulders. "He told us all about it, Ben, so don't try to deny it. We went to see him and he told us everything. How you helped him – saved his life. And the freight cards. You've done it – you're part of the gang – for real this time."

They celebrated by baking potatoes and drinking some cider Paul had smuggled in. Ben thought it tasted foul, making his stomach burn, but he didn't show his discomfort. And when Terry offered him another cigarette, again he refused. Somehow, he felt so much stronger now. He no longer believed he had anything to prove. The incident in the marshalling yard had seen to that. Terry frowned, looked at the cigarette in his hand, then, without a word, he crushed it in his fist and threw it away. The empty packet soon followed. "That's my last one of those," he declared with feeling.

Ben smiled to himself. Another little victory for common sense, he mused. He juggled a piping hot potato from right hand to left, and caught Neville staring at him. He tried a smile, but there was no reciprocation. Later, Paul gathered everyone together and told them they were going to do some more digging. Ben found himself at the back of the press of boys, but not alone. Neville stood beside him and then, when everyone else appeared preoccupied with their tasks, he yanked Ben backwards by the sleeve. His breath stank as he pressed his face close to Ben's. "I can't call you a wimp anymore," he said quietly, "but you'll always be a wimp. And when I find out how you did it, I'll make you pay."

"How I did what, Nev?" Ben pulled his arm free. "What's the problem? You think I cheated, is that it? Of course, you never cheat, do you Nev? I mean, it wouldn't be right to give someone an extra strong cigarette, would it... or cut through a rope swing with a knife?"

Neville gaped at him, his rage boiling over. "How did you fathom that out, you little shit?"

Ben tilted his head. "So, you really did do it."

A volcano seemed to erupt inside the bully's body and his left hand shot out, clamping itself around Ben's throat as his right came back, readied to deliver a punch. But Ben was no longer the wimp so many believed him to be. In reality, he never was, and perhaps Neville should have realized that. Now, it was too late. Ben twisted away, turning his neck against the weakest part of Neville's hand, his thumb. With the hold broken, Neville, caught off balance, teetered backwards slightly and before he could react, Ben had struck him in the face with the point of his elbow.

Ben moved forward, alert, putting all of his force into the next blow, a second elbow strike across the nose.

Shrieking, Neville fell to the ground, his nose leaking blood, his eyes watery and dazed, unable to focus properly. As the pain arrived, his hands came up to his face, the sight of the blood bringing the first despairing, guttural cries from the back of his throat.

Ben studied him, waiting, breathing easy and controlled, hands hanging loosely by his sides.

Neville clambered unsteadily to his feet. He gazed in disbelief at the back of his hand, with the blood spotting, dripping from his nostrils. Shaking, his face came up, twisted in rage, fists bunched, teeth gnashing, voice screaming, "I'll kill you," and made to attack. But Paul loomed between them. Swivelling his hips, he drove his left fist hard into Neville's ribs, doubling the bully up, the air rushing from his lungs, then swung his right square into Neville's jaw. Smashed back down to the earth again, Neville lay there dazed for a brief moment, before rolling over onto his front. He steadied himself like a sprinter waiting for the starting gun to begin the race, then sped off as fast as he could, without words or looks or anything, just the desire flee from the ignominy delivered to him by his two assailants.

"Are you all right?"

Ben stood, watching his tormentor disappearing into the distance, and gave Paul a single nod. "Never better."

There was no point in concerning themselves with the vanquished Neville. "Come on," said Paul, "we've still got those steps to clear."

They returned to their labours, digging away to reveal what lay beneath the soil. As the day drew on, they forgot all about Neville and what happened, except at one point when, breaking off to drink squash, Paul came over and sat down next to Ben. He peered at him keenly and said, "Where did you learn to do that?"

In the middle of gulping down his juice, Ben smacked his lips, gasping. "Learn what?"

"To fight like that? What you did to Neville, the way you broke away then hit him. I've never seen anything like that."

"I don't know – it just sort of flashed into my head."

"Using your elbows – it was like something a commando would do."

"A commando?"

"Yeah, special soldiers who go on secret operations, working behind enemy lines, killing sentries, blowing up bridges."

"I wouldn't know the first thing about how to blow up a bridge."

"No, maybe not, but you know how to look after yourself – like a commando."

Ben lowered his gaze, studying the ground at his feet. "Special Operations Executive," he said in a faraway voice.

"What?"

Coming out of his reverie, Ben looked up to find the others, all gazing at him with new found respect. "Sorry, just talking," said Ben feebly and got to his feet, feeling a little uncomfortable about the direction the conversation was taking. He couldn't begin to understand the things that were happening to him, the brewing confidence, belief in his abilities, the strength surging through his limbs. Since the incident in the marshes, his self-esteem had catapulted. He realized he possessed so many hidden abilities, and strengths to fall back on. The knowledge made him at once pleased but also nervous. Perhaps more problems would follow, for he did not doubt Neville could allow his disgrace to go unavenged.

Resuming their digging, after a few more hours they managed to reveal an entire staircase descending towards a wall of piled up rubble.

Ben paused. Turning towards the top of the steps, he squinted at the sunlight and for a moment, he believed the mysterious soldier stood there, hands on hips, urging him on in silent encouragement.

"Come on," said Ben, his anticipation at what might lay beyond the rubble at fever pitch, "let's get to it."

Hefting his pick-ax, he attacked the mass of broken rocks with renewed vigour and soon, laughing, yelping, driving each other on, the rest joined in. The end was now in sight.

Not so far away, skulking behind a clump of tangled bushes, Neville sat, pinching the bridge of his nose hard to stem the flow of blood. The tears had stopped now. They were not, as Ben would have known, tears of pain, but tears of shame. And with them a brooding, rumbling desire for revenge. He'd got the better of Paul when they'd locked horns before, but Paul had taken him by surprise this time. All because of snivelling Ben's trick. How had he done that, Neville wondered. A little squirt, that's all he was, to move the way he did, hitting him so hard and with such precision. He must have been taking lessons, but not from his dad. No, not his dad – because Ben didn't have one, the little shit. So who was it?

Ruminating on who the suspects might be, Neville took his fingers away from his nose and studied the spots of black blood. "However and wherever," he mumbled aloud, "I'm going to kill him." Ben had probably learned the move from a book, or a magazine, and he'd learned well. Paul's punches were hard, but not as hard as Ben's elbow strikes. No one fought like that. No one.

Neville leaned over and spat into the dirt. He'd bettered Paul once and knew he could do it again. This time, he would show no mercy, and he'd beat him to a pulp with no bloody copper there to help save him. With Paul out of the way, Neville would re-assert his control over the gang and force them to go against that nasty little wimp, Ben. Then he'd punch him senseless, fancy fighting tricks or not. Simple.

He stood up, feeling much better and moved forward. His eyes searched the ground and there, half buried in the earth, lay a forgotten spade. With instant clarity, he knew what it was he had to do.

Chapter Fourteen

A metal door, large and green with a massive, rust-encrusted yet solid looking handle, barred their way.

"We'll never get it open," said Ben, wiping the sweat from his brow, shoulders sagging, the enormity of the task ahead crushing him.

"Yes we will." Paul stepped forward, seized the handle and, grunting with the effort, the veins in his neck bulging, he strained to move it. Two others joined him, but it proved useless, almost as if it were welded shut. Gasping, Paul stepped away, "We'll soak it in oil, then come back tomorrow," he said through clenched teeth.

"My dad's got a can of rust remover," said Trevor.

"Can you get it?" asked Paul. Trevor smiled and nodded. "Then go on then, and be bloody quick about it." Without hesitation, Trevor ran off. Paul scanned the others, waiting there in breathless anticipation of what lay beyond the door. "Come on, the more we chip away the easier it will be when he gets back."

They set to it, hammering away at the rust, filing off the most jagged areas, making so much noise none of them heard the cry of alarm in the distance. Ben noticed it first, stopped and turned. "Something's happened."

Paul held up his hands. The others stopped.

It came again, a drawn out wail and Ben threw down his pick axe and dashed off, the others close behind.

Trevor was on his knees, next to Paul's tunnel. Dragging a hand over a face wet with sweat, Ben walked over. Something was wrong. He didn't know what and his eyes roamed over the surrounding ground, feeling sure someone was close. But he saw nothing, only the thick, lush bushes. Trees. Grass. Nothing unusual. But with every step closer, the awfulness of what lay ahead came into greater clarity. He felt a chill running through him. "Paul," he shouted as loud as he could. "Paul, come here, quick."

They came at a run and stood beside the tunnel, the one Paul had worked so hard on, was so proud of. The perfectly cut batons and beams that supported the roof, the smoothed walls, the even ground. It was all gone. Destroyed. Someone had taken a spade to it and obliterated the entire structure.

Paul stood silent, pale-faced, lips trembling. A single tear rolled down his cheek, but no words followed. Everyone stared, transfixed, stunned.

"Paul."

That single word, spoken so softly, barely audible, but instantly recognizable.

Neville's voice.

"I did that, Paul. And I enjoyed it."

Paul turned to face his adversary, the perpetrator of this desecration, fists already bunching, the inevitable confrontation about to start.

But nothing went as expected.

Neville hit him square in the jaw with the handle of the spade, a violent thrust, hard enough to fell a bull.

It felled Paul with ease, dropping him like a stone.

A stunned silence followed. Then someone moaned.

Paul lay there, face a mess of blood, eyes wide open, gazing skywards in disbelief. One or two of the boys whimpered in alarm, another laughed.

Ben alone remained still and quiet, measuring Neville, waiting for the big bully to turn on him.

But Neville brought the spade down to his side, as if it were a rifle and he were a soldier coming to attention. He smiled a sweet and sickly smile, titling his head, "That was easy," he said.

Ben nodded. At a rough guess, he would have said that Neville measured nine, perhaps ten inches taller than him. Almost fully grown. Strong too. But that wouldn't matter. Because he knew what to do.

He flexed his knees, feet turning inwards slightly.

"Wait," came a voice to him, a calm and reassuring voice, a voice he knew. "Put your opponent off guard, smile, do not cause him unease. Don't allow him to think you are about to attack. Then, when he relaxes and takes his eyes from you, that is when you strike. And you strike hard and true, without holding anything back. Believe in yourself, in your abilities, and centre on what you must do. Any hesitation, the moment will pass, the opportunity lost, and he will recover and he will prevail." Ben listened, eyes closing briefly, before he looked at Neville and smiled. "Yes Nev," he said, "it was very easy. But that's because you always knew you'd win. Like we all did. Even me."

Neville frowned. "Really?" He gave a little laugh. "You really thought that?"

"Of course. I've always known you could take Paul. I don't think you needed the spade, either."

Neville shook his head, "You know what, wimpy, I think I might go a little easy on you. Maybe just hit you six times, instead of ten."

Someone laughed. Neville laughed. Trevor said, "Ben, what the hell …"

Then Ben too laughed, the sound causing Neville to frown again, his voice changing tone, growing dangerous. "I'm going to beat the living shit out of you," the bully said.

Trevor stepped forward, arms raised, "Nev, come on, you don't have to do this. I'll take Ben home and we'll never—"

A single straight left into the nose shut Trevor up for the next few moments, and he cart wheeled over to his left, hitting the ground hard, and burst into tears.

Ben watched his friend, fighting back the urge to go to him. His hands came up, surrendering. "Please," he said, voice tremulous, eyes filling with tears, "please Nev, don't hurt me." Bringing his trembling hands together, it looked as though he were praying, not begging.

"You'll have to beg harder than that," cackled Neville, laughing loudly, turning in triumph to his captivated audience. "This is going to be more fun than I ever imagined possible."

Later, when it was over, if anyone had asked the witnesses to describe what they had seen, none of them would have been able to recount it in perfect detail. It was just too quick. One moment Ben was clasping his hands together, palm against palm, then those same hands were moving with such speed it was as if they were being driven by some form of machinery. Two strikes and Neville went down, his big frame no defence against such perfectly delivered blows. The solar plexus, then the right temple, the final strike dumping Neville unceremoniously into the dirt. It was all over, as quickly and as simply as that, and Ben had barely broken sweat.

Ben stood quiet for a few moments, his eyes not focusing. Where had that skill come from, that knowledge of how to hit someone like that? A three-fingered strike, a swinging elbow. The voice guiding him, filling him with such overwhelming confidence, such complete control of his actions. There was no fear, no self- doubt, just a desire to do what was required.

And now, it was over. Neville sprawled out, unconscious. Paul beside him, Trevor whimpering, clutching his face.

Ben took it all in, detached, cold. Soon, word would spread about what he'd done. To defeat someone as big and as strong as Neville, with such ease. Some would treat him as a hero, others as a freak, a hard case, or any combination of those things. Fairly soon, others would be squaring up to him. Others bigger and harder than Neville, out to prove they could do better. There were plenty of them out there.

Or maybe not, he mused. Maybe he could just ignore it, keep a low profile, walk away. As he always had done in the past.

But things were different now.

He'd shown himself to be someone. Someone who stood up. From now on, no one would allow him to be quiet, aloof, alone.

No one.

From way off in the distance, the sound of approaching sirens shattered the silence. In a blink, the gang broke into a desperate stampede, pounding across Darley Dene towards the boundary wall.

With the sirens drawing closer, Ben watched them run and knew it was all for the best. Their garbled, disjointed stories would only complicate things. Keep it simple. That was his new motto.

He went across to Trevor first, putting his arm around him, holding him tight.

"Shit, Ben," his friend said, voice cracking, "is that the police?"

"Probably. Ambulance too I shouldn't wonder. I reckon Nev called them, knowing what he was going to do."

"I think he broke my nose."

Cupping his friend's face in both hands, Ben studied his bruised and bloody features. "Maybe. They'll fix you up, and no running off this time."

"My leg's still hurting. Now this. Mum's never going to let me out of the house again."

Ben sniggered. "That might be for the best, after what's gone on here today."

A moan caused him to look over to the others. Neville. Face ashen, sat upright, coughing hoarsely. He spat a globule of blood into the ground.

Leaving Trevor behind, Ben sauntered over to the defeated bully. "Listen to me," he said.

Neville looked up into Ben's eyes and groaned. "What the hell did you do to me?"

"I hit you. Twice. I'll hit you again if you don't listen."

Face draining of colour, Neville pushed himself backwards. "No, please – don't do that."

"You made the call, didn't you, to the police?"

"I didn't think you'd—"

"Let me just tell it as I see it. Feel free to butt-in any time you want." He took in a deep breath. "You were going to put it all on me, weren't you? Tell the police I hit Paul with the spade, get me sent to court, get done for GBH?" Neville nodded, breath coming in short gasps. "I thought as much. You'd get all the gang to vouch for you, probably add in the bit where you had to beat me up to stop me from doing any more damage to Paul." He shook his head. "Well, as it's an emergency call, they'll want answers, and they'll want to know why Paul's face is in such a mess – and who did it, and why."

With mouth open, saliva drooling, Neville appeared confused, bewildered, and a little afraid.

"He was in the tunnel," said Ben with unsettling assurance, "it collapsed, we had to drag him out. That's it, the story we tell."

Neville frowned. "I – I don't understand."

"The story we tell the police. Paul was in there," he pointed to the collapsed tunnel, "and we had to dig him out. That's why he's in such a mess."

"Whatever you say."

And when the police did finally arrive and the ambulance took Trevor and Paul away to the hospital, they recounted their story, the one they rehearsed, the one concocted by Ben.

"Looks like he wasn't the only one who got hurt," said one of the officers, ticking them both off with his forefinger. "Had a falling out have we?"

"It was my fault," said Ben quickly. "No one knew what to do, and we argued. We came to blows, but nothing serious."

"Bit of a boxer, are you?"

"A bit."

Convinced, the policeman allowed them to go and visit Paul's mum and tell her what had happened and why Paul wouldn't be coming home that night. She listened in stunned silence then grabbed her coat and rushed off to the hospital.

Making their way back home, Ben said, "Neither of us will ever be able to tell the truth."

"No-one else will say anything," said Neville through clenched teeth. "Neither will Paul."

"I know he won't."

They stopped yards away from Ben's front door. It was growing dark and Ben knew his mum would be angry again. He gave Neville a look. "I know you still hate me," he said.

"I'll always hate you," said Neville. "This isn't over."

"I know that too," Ben replied, opened the gate and pressed the bell.

Chapter Fifteen

Mum was out so it was Nan who gave him a hard time about being out so late. Ben waited until the fusillade of screaming and shouting subsided before he explained, as briefly as he could, what had happened. He stuck to the agreed lie, but at the mention of the green door in Darley Dene, Nan's expression changed, anger replaced by a wide-eyed look, which, if pressed, Ben would probably describe as 'terror'. But terror of what? Nan slumped in her chair at the kitchen table and stared into space for a moment.

"Oh Ben," she said at last, her voice sounding tired. "When are you ever going to start doing as you're told?"

"Nan, there's nothing there except—"

"No, Ben there is something there. Something you can't understand."

"Well why don't you explain it to me then?"

She shook her head, "I don't think it's my place...It should be up to your mother."

"You've said that before," Ben reached forward, taking her hands in his, "Nan, please, I need to know...things have been...happening to me, things I can't explain."

"Things? What sort of things?"

"Voices mostly. Telling me how to do stuff, things I never knew I could do."

"Ben, you need to tell me everything. What have you been doing down in Darley Dene?"

He stared into her eyes, reluctant to begin, but knowing he must. He recounted everything – the rope swing, the tunnel, the fight with Neville, the steps, and finally the door. The only part he didn't tell was the truth of what happened to Paul.

Nan listened without re-action, her eyes never leaving his. When he finished, she reached out and gripped his hand with surprising strength. "You mustn't try and go through that door, Ben. I want you to promise me."

"Nan, you have to tell me why you're so worried. What are you afraid of? Is there something in there, an ammunition store or something? Something dangerous?"

"Something dangerous, yes. But not ammunition."

"What then?"

She nodded, eyes hardening, reaching a decision. "It should be your Mum – but, all right, I'll tell you." She sat back, staring into the distance, into the memory of years gone by. "During the War, the Blitz, we'd get under the stairs and all huddle together when the air-raids came. Christmas 1940 was one of the worst. An incendiary came through our upstairs front window. We managed to put it out, but only just. Lots of people helped one another back then, the Blitz bringing everyone together. We never stopped living out our lives. We'd still go to work, the shops, brush our steps, go out at night for a drink – even when there was an air-raid on. It was like we were telling Hitler exactly what he could do with his bloomin' bombs." She sniggered. "Your Mum was like that – she never worried about anything, just got on with it. She had a little dog called Trudy. We built an air-raid shelter for her in the back garden and she'd run into it when she heard the bombers coming over. She'd hear them before the sirens went off, and we'd know a raid was close. We'd get the mattress ready and get under the stairs. Thankfully, a real bomb never hit us. A landmine blew a whopping big hole in the street, but that was further up. Killed poor old Mr. Gordon, the baker. Silly man was poking his head out of the window watching the damned thing as it floated down on its parachute...terrible it was. No, we just blundered through, I suppose you could say. We just...got on with things.

"Your Mum would go out most weekends with either her friend Miriam or your aunty Ida. One Saturday – or it might have been a Friday, I can't remember – she brought back some soldiers to the house. Lovely lads they were. We all sat in the front room...I can see them now. Then a raid began, like nothing you could imagine. The worst one yet. We all got under the stairs. Second week of March, 1941, the beginning of a whole series of nightly raids. They seemed to go on forever."

She paused, biting down on her bottom lip. Ben leaned forward. "Nan, you don't need to—"

"I'm all right," she said with a smile. "Memories can be difficult at times." She sucked in a breath. "Well, this particular night, it seemed like the whole sky was lit up – like daytime. The poor lads were terrified, but of the raid or something else, I couldn't be sure. Then someone was pounding on the door. The lads thought it was their sergeant, come to get them. They were billeted down in Darley Dene, you see, which served as an army camp back then. Lots of soldiers were camped there, right by the docks. Anyway, it wasn't their sergeant. It was poor old Billy Gates, the air-raid warden. Poor bloke was shaking like a leaf. We let him in and he sat in the corner, huddled up and trembling, puffing on his cigarette, never saying a word. None of us laughed, all of us scared to death. All of us.

"It was too dangerous for the soldiers to try and get back to the barracks, so we persuaded them to stay the night. When the bombing finally stopped, Billy went back to duty and we all tried to sleep, but none of us could. There were fires everywhere, and fire engines were roaring backwards and forwards. It was the most horrible night I've ever known. Anyway, as soon as it was light, the soldiers made their way back to Darley Dene. But as we stood at the door to wave them off, we could see something wasn't right. There were more bells clanging from all over the place. Fire engines, ambulances, racing down the street, people shouting. Your mum and I ran down to see what on earth was going on. As we ran, the whole sky glowed bright orange. We knew it was the docks. They must have taken a terrible pounding in the night, and when we got there, we saw it – cranes, warehouses, ships. They had all been hit. There were fires everywhere. But there was something else as well. The boys – the soldiers – they were standing there, stiff as boards, their eyes wide, black rimmed, not really looking at anything. In shock, we learned later, because of what they had seen. It was the camp, you see. Darley Dene. It had taken a series of direct hits and the men there, the soldiers… many had been killed, even more wounded. Some were buried in the rubble of their underground shelters, shelters which did nothing to protect them. We learned later that the emergency services tried desperately to dig the survivors out, but it was a terrible job. They worked throughout the day, but had to abandon their efforts when the Germans came again that evening.

"Your mum and I went around in a daze for weeks on end. It kept racing through our minds: if we hadn't persuaded those soldiers to stay, they would almost certainly be dead. That was a…disturbing idea, Ben. Made you really think about lots of things. Fate. Life and death. How nothing is permanent, how a single deed can alter everything, in an instant. Everything.

"A few days later, the boys came to see us again. They were on charges for being AWOL – absent without leave. The police – military police – came to speak with us and we told them exactly what had happened. Billy Gates came forward and gave his testimony. Cost him his job, poor chap, but he was never really suited to it. He even thanked us." She shook her head, a thin smile spreading over her face. "Poor Billy. He dropped down dead two months later. Doctor said it was delayed shock. Can you believe that?"

"What happened to the soldiers, Nan?"

A deep sigh. "Our statements meant they dropped all charges against the boys. We became good friends. More than friends, if truth be told. Your mum and one of them became close. Very close, Ben. Over the next few months, things developed. They fell in love.

"Then, totally out of the blue, he got transferred. They had to as his original unit had been…well, destroyed. Your mum's boyfriend, he got sent away for special training. He kept in touch, but his officers censored all his letters, so he couldn't say very much. Someone had scratched out most of what he had written. He was a sort of commando, he said, receiving secret training. Anyway, the last we heard from him was they'd sent him to North Africa on what he called 'special operations'. Your mum never heard from him again. Months of heartbreak followed until eventually she couldn't take it anymore and she went over to Liverpool; the War Office had some office over there. She went to see if there was any news. They wouldn't tell her, of course, because she wasn't a relative. But when she told them what had happened, how they were planning on marrying, they relented. That's when she learned he'd been killed, whilst on active duty.

"I remember when she came home. She was like a little girl again. I held her all through the night, and most of the next few days. She just cried and cried and cried. But, there was one thing, one thing that was to keep his memory alive. The one thing she was to treasure for always, and the only thing that got her through the whole terrible mess."

Nan stood up with an effort and went over to fill the kettle. Ben watched her, waiting for something more, but she didn't seem to have anything left to say. She put a match to the gas ring and delicately placed the kettle on the hob. Everything done with methodical slowness, as if she wanted to keep her mind firmly fixed on what she was doing, that even the simple act of making a pot of tea was better than doing nothing. Because then she would have to remember some more, say something more. And clearly, she didn't want to do that.

But Ben knew the story wasn't ended. He went over to Nan and gently put his hand on her shoulder. "Nan. What was the treasure?"

When she turned to look at him, her eyes were smiling, but filled with tears. "Oh Ben," she said quietly and reached out to touch his cheek with such a show of affection that Ben too almost cried. "It's you. You're the treasure. He was your dad."

Chapter Sixteen

When the shaking brought him awake, he sat upright, rubbing his eyes, Mum standing before him, breathing hard, red-faced. Not angry. Incensed. He immediately thought Nan had told her about the incident down at Darley Dene.

"Mum, what's—"

She rammed the photograph into his face. "Where did you get this?"

He blinked, brain fuzzy with sleep, squinting at the image wangled before his eyes. He'd completely forgotten about it. The photograph he'd picked up during that night at the tattoo. Without thinking he'd put it into his jeans, before putting them in the laundry basket last night. She must have found it when she was sorting out the clothes, but why was she so angry? "Mum, I didn't think you'd—"

Her eyes narrowed, "How dare you go through my things," she said venomously. "You have no right, no right to even be in my room – do you understand?"

Mouth dropping open, he held up his hands, "Mum, I promise you, I didn't."

"You bloody little liar," she spat and, gripping the edge of the blanket, she flicked the photograph into his face and stormed off.

Stunned, Ben gazed at the faded image lying there next to him. It was the closest she had ever come to hitting him. She'd never spoken to him like that before. In a daze, he stumbled out of bed, body shaking, fighting back the tears.

Nan was at the kitchen sink, washing the mandatory dishes, when Ben came in. She stopped, a pained expression developing across her face. "Ben," she said quietly, "what were you thinking?"

"*Thinking?*" He blew out his cheeks, the anger welling up. "I haven't done anything, for God's sake! She comes in, screaming and shouting as if I'd committed a crime or something."

"*She?* Who is 'she'?" She dried her hands on a tea towel and hurled it away into the corner. "You had a photograph, Ben, a photograph she cherished and she found it in your jeans. What angers me more than anything is that you took it after I'd told you about what happened. You went through her things and found the one thing – the *one thing* that would tell her you know something. And the only way you could know something was because someone had told you. And that some-one must be me." She brought down both her fists on the table with such force the little glass conduit-set standing in the centre rattled and toppled over. She loomed forward. "That was a sinful thing to do, Ben."

Without giving him the chance to offer up any sort of explanation, she stormed out. He reeled at her words, shuddered and slumped into his chair. In the space of just a few minutes, he had upset the two most important people in his world.

It was a deadly dull day, the sky iron grey, all of it making his dark mood even heavier as he trudged into town. Head down, hands thrust deep into his pockets, feeling like a fool. He knew he shouldn't. It wasn't his fault. He should have stood up and explained, but he had had no chance and now his mum had gone off to work with the tears pouring down her cheeks. He knew he would have to tell her, but he didn't really know where to begin. How could she understand, how could she believe any of it? In fact, in the cold light of day, did he really believe it? Any of it?

The shops were quiet, a few dreary customers idly looking through the shelves. He headed for the only two places he found any joy. The 'Hobby Shop' and the local booksellers. Ben loved to read. Unfortunately, because he did not receive pocket money, he couldn't afford to buy anything. He once suggested being a paperboy, but Mum emphatically forbade him; she did not want him cycling around the town in the cold, bleak mornings of winter, in the dark. She'd told him, if there was anything he wanted, he only had to ask. Ben rarely did. He knew money was tight, so the only thing left to him was window-shopping.

With nose pressed against the glass, taking in the wonderful array of toys and models, thoughts turned to Trevor, of their long days playing together. He really should go and visit his friend, make sure he was all right after the horrors of the previous few days. At least he would be in the company of someone who would understand, who would listen.

Making up his mind to go right there and then, he turned to see the one thing he truly did not want to see.

Neville.

The big lout emerged from the rear entrance of Woollies, preoccupied with cramming his mouth with handfuls of crisps. Ben took his chance and, with head down, slinked away in the opposite direction.

"Hey, Wimpy!"

Ben winced, but kept going, not daring to look up. But all that changed when Neville came bounding up and grabbed him by the arm.

"Hiya, Benny-boy, what you doin'?"

Ben scowled. Neville seemed cheerful enough, relaxed, busying himself with sucking the last remnants of salt and grease from his fingertips. He threw the empty crisp packet onto the floor. Ben watched the wind take it up and send it on a twisting journey down the street. How he longed to be that empty packet at that moment.

"You'll never guess what," continued Neville, wiping his hands on his jeans. He laughed loudly, and frowned at Ben's silence. "Don't you wanna know?"

"What?" said Ben in a tired voice, accepting that Neville would not go until the secrets were spilled.

Neville leaned closer to him, as if entering into a great conspiracy. "We opened the door."

The words struck home like blows. Ben did a double take. "The door? You opened the door?"

Neville nodded his head like some demented bobbing toy so often seen on the rear shelf of cars. "Yeah, that's right. We did what Paul said – packed the handle with oil and grease, left it for ages, then got stuck into it with chisels and screw-drivers."

"Wow," said Ben, impressed. "Did you go inside?"

Neville grinned, "Not really. I took a step in, but it was too dark – I mean, it was *black*. We're going to get some torches and go back later this saffy. You going to come down?"

"You want me to?"

Neville shrugged, "Wouldn't be tellin' you if I didn't, would I?" He grinned. "Look, no hard feelings, eh? Just get down there, around four. Okay?"

Ben nodded feebly and Neville playfully punched him in the arm, then he was gone, laughing to himself as he went, leaving Ben to wonder if it was all true, or another of the bully's tricks.

Returning home, he found Nan sitting in her room, radio on, knitting yet another scarf, sipping her tea. Ben tentatively knocked on her door and went in, sitting down on the sofa next to her. She didn't flinch, just kept on knitting. "I'm sorry, Nan," he said quietly.

She put down the brightly coloured scarf, careful not to allow the needles to slip out of the stitching, and took a sip of tea. It always fascinated him at the amount of wool she went through creating scarves, gloves and goodness knows what, for nobody in particular. She looked at him, reading his thoughts. "What are you staring at?"

"Nothing."

"Guilty conscience? You should have."

"But I didn't do anything, Nan."

"Then where did you get the photograph from?"

Ben looked away. What would be the point in telling her, she wouldn't believe him. Even if she did, she'd just get angry again, accuse him of lying and the whole thing would have come round in one great big circle.

"I thought as much," she said and got to her feet. "What troubles me," she said, picking up her teacup and saucer, "is not so much what you did, which is pretty dreadful anyway, but how you knew where to look. You must have been in your Mum's room lots of times, sneaking about."

"No, Nan I—"

She held up her hand like a policeman stopping traffic, "I don't want to hear your voice, Ben. Not only did you know where to look, but you also knew what to take. Of all the things…" She shook her head, anger receding. "I blame those boys you hang around with, them and that bloody place you keep going to."

"Darley Dene?"

"I asked you to keep away, didn't I?" Her anger returned, her face reddening. "But you couldn't. You can never, ever do as you're told, can you? Two of your friends have been hurt, one seriously, you nearly drowned in that marsh, and now all of this spiteful, spiteful business with the photograph – you've nearly broken your Mum's heart, Ben. I hope you're very happy with yourself. If it were up to me I'd give you a bloody good hiding, I would."

She stormed out, angrier than Ben had ever seen her. He sat there, bunching his fists, feeling so inadequate, so trapped.

Darley Dene…damn Darley Dene!

Chapter Seventeen

It was a brighter day as Ben walked away from his friend's house. Not because of the weather, which was still dismal, but because he found Trevor in such good spirits. A painful anti-tetanus injection meant he still couldn't go out, but his leg and face were both on the mend. Laid up in bed, radio on full blast, drinking Ovaltine and eating digestive biscuits, his eyes sparkled with contentment. Ben couldn't help smiling as he left.

Strolling along the winding path curled away from Trevor's door, Ben paused to gaze towards the railways embankment and, there on the far side, Darley Dene. Lost in thought, his smile faded. Perhaps his Nan was right. Nothing but trouble had come his way since that first exploration of Darley Dene. And now, with so much more of its mysteries being literally unearthed, the time might be here for him to turn his back on it, leaving it and the bad memories far behind.

Even as the idea formulated in his mind, the truth refused to budge. He knew, if nothing else, whatever Neville and the others had revealed in their frenzied digging, Ben needed to know. Hefting his shoulders, he put his head down and slowly tramped down the path towards Darley Dene.

The hands on Saint Luke's church clock tower eased past four o'clock and Ben pulled in a deep breath, wondering Neville and his cronies would be there. What he'd said earlier might be just another trick, of course. A ploy to lure Ben into yet another of Neville's humiliating games.

His fears vanished, however, as he clambered over the wall. Dropping to the ground on the other side, Neville and the others were rushing towards him, broad grins of their eager face. As Neville drew closer, Ben experienced a strange sense of elation at seeing him. And when the big bully slapped Ben good-heartedly on the shoulder, happiness replaced trepidation.

Jabbering away to one another, the boys crowded around, full of excitement. Neville doled out cigarettes, Ben the only one who declined.

Neville sneered. For a moment, charged resentment reappeared, but Ben, quick as anything, popped a piece of American chewing gum into his mouth and winked. "I got these instead."

They all stopped and watched him working his jaws around the gum with an almost maniacal glee. Even Neville, who moments earlier seemed about to blurt out something sarcastic and spiteful, gaped as Ben blew out an enormous pink bubble.

"How do you do *that*," he gasped, unable to tear his eyes away.

"Easy," said Ben and placed another piece of gum into the big bully's hand, "I'll show you if you like."

Neville's came up from the gum. "Really?"

"Really."

Without warning, Neville threw away his cigarette and tore away the outer wrapper to the gum. He popped the stick into his mouth and tried, in abject failure, to blow his own bubble. Embarrassed, cheeks reddening, he said, "It must have taken a lot of practice."

Continuing to chomp on the gum, Ben shrugged, "No, not much. I …" He stopped, a curious tingling sensation playing around at the back of his neck, forcing him to ask himself how and when he'd learned that trick.

"Anyway," said Neville, breaking into Ben's thoughts, "let's take a look at what we've found."

The solid metal door stood slightly ajar. "None of us have had a look yet," said Neville, his eyes wide as he peered into the gloom beyond. "We think it's a shelter."

"Yes," said Ben, his voice breathless, full of anticipation, "I think that too."

One of the others stepped up and handed Neville a small, battery torch. Neville looked down and his fingers slowly wrapped around its silver-coloured casing. "Thanks Richard."

Richard stepped back and for a long moment, no one moved.

"Come on," said Neville suddenly, breaking the heavy silence. He pressed down on the torch button and a thin beam of light sprang out from its front. He played it over the dull, metal door. "I'll go in first, then Ben you follow. The rest of you, wait here until I call you in." As a collective gasp of relief trickled out from the others, Neville pushed his way through the gap and Ben followed.

It was a grim and fearful place, the ghosts of the past very evident in the eerie darkness, coupled with the over-powering smell of damp and decay. The thin torchlight barely cut through the blackness as Neville played the beam in every direction, picking out piles of debris here and there. Rocks, upturned crates, jumbles of jagged metal, blankets, old, discarded cans, and masses of broken timber. The whole place was a mess. It also stank, the thick tang of dampness catching the back of Ben's throat. Reaching out, he ran his palm over the nearest wall. It was dripping wet.

"God, what a place," exhaled Neville, not daring to raise his voice above a whisper. He moved forward, and when his foot crunched down on something, he stopped.

"What is it?" Ben stepped closer, squinting through the gloom. His eyes were slowly adjusting to the lack of light, but objects continued to be nothing more than vague shapes.

"It's an old box," said Neville. "It's got some writing across the lid, but I – wait, I'll try and read what it says ..." He grunted and stooped down, training the torch over the surface. "It's too faded. Maybe the damp, or rain or something has worn it all away. Have a look."

But Ben, squinting hard, could not make out a thing. "Bring the light up," he hissed, "You're not directing it on the right part.

Neville swung the beam straight into Ben's face, who gasped, stumbling backwards, hands instinctively coming up to shield his face.

"Jesus!"

"Sorry, Ben," said Neville in a sing-song voice.

Within a blink, it became evident Neville was very far from being sorry. Temporarily blinded, Ben didn't see the punch until it slammed into his guts, doubling him up, sending him retching and spluttering to his knees.

"Sniveling little toad," snarled Neville, pressing his mouth close to Ben's ear. "Think you could get one over on me? Took me by surprise you did, you shit. It's not going to happen again, wimpy boy, not to me."

From somewhere, Ben felt the rush of wind, but before he could doge or swerve, Neville's boot cracked into his ribs. A blinding stab of pain, and he pitched over, curling himself up, crying out. A rough hand took him by the collar, half lifting him, and a heavy fist struck hard against his jaw and he fell down, writhing in the filth. Breathing came in short, stabbing bursts, each intake bringing more pain from his ribs. They must be broken, a thought that brought fear. He managed a pathetic, "Please..." before everything went black.

For a moment Ben thought unconsciousness had conquered him but then, as he struggled to sit up, biting back the tears, he saw the last sliver of the light from the door as Neville pulled open. Silhouetted against the afternoon daylight, his mocking, taunting voice rang out, "Enjoy yourself, wimpy." Then the heavy, metal door swung shut with a great clanging sound and the blackness became total.

The silence enveloped him, utter disbelief consumed him. This couldn't be true. He must be unconscious, dreaming what Neville had done. No one could be so callous, so heartless.

He sat up, tenderly rubbing his jaw, the only sound that of his laboured, ragged breathing. His only companion the throbbing pain in both jaw and ribs.

And as he sat, and the reality worked its way into his brain, the realization of the predicament facing him almost became too much and, clamping both hands over his mouth, he let loose a prolonged wail of abject horror.

Neville had locked him in.

Chapter Eighteen

With the darkness pressing in all around, he tried his best to remain calm, convincing himself this was another test, another ordeal to cement Neville's superiority. There was no way they would leave him in there, alone, afraid. They'd open the door soon, when the joke had worn a little thin and Neville, assured that Ben's punishment had been a fitting one, would stand and gloat. Soon. They'd open the door soon. Surely...

But how long was 'soon'? Five minutes, ten? Half an hour? The more Ben thought the more he could feel the panic rising.

Rubbing his face and, pleased to discover the pain had receded from his jawline, took a deep breath before crawling, inch by painful inch, through the stinking wet floor towards the door. First his left hand, then his right, outstretched, feeling his way forward, guessing which direction to take, disorientated, smothered in darkness.

A sudden thought gave him a glimmer of optimism. Maybe it wouldn't be locked. Maybe, if he could put his shoulder against it, he could force the door open.

His hand touched the wall and he jerked it back at the shock of its cold wetness. He must have veered away from his chosen path by accident. He took a moment, steadying himself, before moving along once again, his hands on the stone, or brick wall, until he came to the much colder and much wetter steel door. Slowly he stood up, waited, gathering himself, then pressed himself against the unforgiving metal with all his might, straining every sinew, gritting his teeth with the effort.

His knees buckled and he slid down to the ground, defeated.

The door remained closed solid.

His head lolled onto his chest and he sat, not daring to accept the enormity of his dilemma. The tears welled up in his eyes. Not tears of pain, for none of that mattered anymore. Total despair made him cry out and he swung around, pummelling the heavy doors with both fists, screaming, "Let me out, *let me out for God's sake!*"

But they didn't.

And as he slid back down, a new, even more terrifying thought gripped him. They weren't going to keep him in there for five minutes, or even five hours. Because as he sat there he could hear them, through the door, laughing and cheering. And they were running away, leaving him inside, to rot away.

Pressing the heels of his palms hard into his eyes, the last vestiges of courage seeped out of him and he succumbed to the horror and wept uncontrollably.

The steady, distant drip of water forced him to sit up. Head back, he sniffed and listened. The sound told him two things. One that the place was far, far bigger than anyone ever imagined, and two, there just might be another way out – a forgotten entrance, or tunnel, or something. Anything. It would be worth a look, if only he could look. If only he had the torch, or a light, or…Ben stopped himself short and gave a little whoop of triumph. Of course he had light – the box of matches he was going to use to light the boys' cigarettes, before he came up with the more effective gum-trick.

He reached into his pocket and felt around the box, opened it and slipped out a match. Some fell to the ground, to sink beneath the oily puddles at his feet. Slowing down, mindful this may be his only chance, he carefully dragged the tip across the abrasive side. It flared into life, illuminating his immediate surroundings for an all too brief flicker of time.

The match went out.

Enveloped in darkness once more, he cried out, the matches spilling over his fumbling fingers.

Scraping around in the filthy ground, trying to keep the mounting panic at bay, he mumbled words of long forgotten prayers. One, single match would do it. He still clutched the box, but what possible use was that if there was nothing to strike against it?

And then his fingers brushed over the unmistakable shape of a match. Holding onto it as if it were the most precious thing in the world, his hand trembled as he brought it towards the box. He paused, knowing he had this one chance remaining. If this match flared and died, he knew he would find no other.

A voice, calm and instantly recognisable, came to him, stopping him in the act of striking.

"Just strike it, Ben," the voice, detached, reverberating around the interior, so assured, filled him with awe. "Strike and you'll see,"

But Ben paused, his mouth open, heart pounding. The voice, at once soothing and calm, also sent a chill through him. Especially in this place. What did it mean, 'you'll see'? Was that a literal phrase, or a pointer to something more sinister? Ben had no idea, nor did he have the luxury of considering the options – there were none. Taking in a breath to try to steady himself, he struck the match.

It flared and lit up his immediate surroundings. Cupping the flame with his other hand, he slowly moved the match around, screwing his eyes up to try and see a way out. But he couldn't see anything, the light from the match too weak to penetrate very far into the gloom. Fearful the tiny flame would soon die, he used the diminishing light to locate more of the fallen matches and bent down to gather them up.

As the light did indeed splutter and fade, he saw something lying on its side, half submerged in the broken ground. All he hoped for now was that it would still work.

Chapter Nineteen

Careful not to stumble over the many lumps of fallen masonry and pieces of sharp, protruding metal, Ben inched forward. In his hand was the old oil lantern he had found half-buried amongst the debris, lighting it with one of his remaining matches. He never stopped to ask himself how the wick remained soaked in paraffin for so many years, but he felt certain the voice had something to do with helping him discover the old, rusted lamp, which spluttered and hissed. Although weak, the glow allowed him to navigate his way ever deeper into the interior of the subterranean passages and, hopefully, a way out.

Stretching before him, at one point the passages branched off into a number of different directions. Ben raised the lantern, trying to reveal what lay within. Most were knee deep in water, and a collapsed roof blocked another. There was little doubt in his mind this was the shelter hit during the bombing raid that Nan described. The thought of so many men dying here brought the most horrible, stomach turning feeling to him and he stopped, debating which way to go, wondering if he had the strength to continue.

It was the cessation of the dripping which caused him to focus and listen with heightened awareness. He stared into the gloom, straining to pick out details, and as he did a series of changes took place, changes to the very air around him.

The walls altered first, becoming a swirling mix of colours and shapes, none of them solid, bricks transforming into an undulating wall of patterns and shades. Right before his eyes the ruined mess of the shelter returned to what it once was - a well ordered, well maintained living area. Cold bare walls replaced with smooth, light plaster, debris on the ground now a swept, wooden floor. The hum of a generator allowed electricity to light up the rooms, revealing bunk beds lining the walls, blankets neatly folded, metal lockers close by. A soft, orange glow covered everything, and Ben's fear, warmed by it, seeped away. It was like watching a film. But one without actors. At least at first.

As he stood, gawping, those very same actors materialized out of nowhere. Initially shadowy and vague, figures slowly took on more substance as they moved around, chatting with each other. Ben heard their voices, their laughter. He watched them walk, flop down on their bunks, open up letters or magazines. A notion of being a spectator gathered force in his mind, borne out by the realization that although he could see them, they could not see him. Ben cried out in alarm as one shirt-sleeved soldier got up from his bunk and walked right through him. Breathless, Ben swung around to watch the man stroll away into the gloom, undisturbed, unaffected.

Thinking that any sudden movement would either bring the visions to an abrupt end or, perhaps more frighteningly, cause the soldiers to re-act at his presence, he moved away to the side and got down on his haunches. Realising he no longer needed the lantern, he turned the flame down and observed all before him.

The soldiers went about their everyday business, some working, others cleansing boots, checking equipment. They chatted, shared jokes, drifted off to sleep. More a drone from a swarm of bees, individual conversations merged into one constant hum. The place was alive with men.

Something from the corner of his eye caught his attention and Ben turned and gave a start. One of the soldiers stood rock still, gazing directly towards him. Ben realized with alarm the soldier quite obviously could see him.

"No-one else is aware of your presence," he said quietly. His eyes were hard and black, his face etched with fatigue. Could he be...?

The man took a breath. "Follow me," he said and turned on his heels. Without a moment's thought, Ben stood up and moved in behind him.

They tramped along another narrow passageway, the ceiling low, forcing the soldier to stoop. Now and then, another uniformed man squeezed past, but not one registered any awareness of either of them.

"How come they can't see me," Ben said.

"You're from the future," said the soldier, without stopping.

"But you can see me. Why is that? Who are you, why are you—"

The soldier stopped and turned. "You don't recognize me?"

Ben thought he did. This close, with the ceiling lights so much more intense, he thought he knew those features. But there was something about him that made Ben doubt this was the same soldier from the tattoo, the one who saved Trevor and him from the shunting yard. "I don't understand," he said. "How can you—"

He got no further.

Without warning, the narrow corridor widened, walls receding, and merged into a much wider area, with maps on the wall, trestle tables with clerks seated behind, punching typewriter keys, officers snapping orders, men milling around. A hub of activity.

Then the lights flickered and dimmed.

For a moment, an eerie, ominous silence fell over everything. Ben tensed and the soldier turned to him. "This is when it happens."

A deep, heavy rumble from somewhere far away, followed by a violent, prolonged shaking broke out. It gradually built into a crescendo of noise, huge, thumping sounds, like steam-hammers, pounding down on the roof. Soldiers screamed, fixtures rattled, objects fell over, cups and plates smashing to the ground.

Ben cried out, frightened, but the soldier held up a finger and pressed it against his lips. Ben stopped. "It's an air raid," said the soldier matter-of-factly, and he directed Ben to watch as the other soldiers scurried about, grabbing helmets and equipment whilst the dreaded sound of falling bombs filled the air.

With the shrill whistle of swiftly descending bombs over-taking everything, Ben went to his knees, hands clamped over his ears, crying out, "Make it stop!"

Massive explosions tore through the confines of the room, bringing down the ceiling, masonry hitting the ground, sending out great clouds of dust and smoke into the air. Men screamed. "Please, for God's sake, make it stop!"

And then it did, almost before the words left his mouth. He waited, breathing hard, sure this was merely a lull, a pause in the nightmare of destruction and death played out all around him.

He took a chance and looked up. The soldier gazed down at him, a half amused expression on his face, right forefinger raised, like a conductor in some horrible symphony of noise and despair.

"I will have my vengeance," hissed the soldier, face twisting into a grimace. "Unless you help me with what I want."

Ben gaped, at a loss to the man's meaning. And the more Ben stared, the more he realised the man's features were changing. Rice-paper like skin, thin, wrinkled, grey, and aged, becoming more so by the second. This was not the same man from the tattoo, this was someone consumed with hatred, anger, a twisted, maligned soul, eaten up by the desire for revenge. But against what, against who?

As he looked, the background seemed to blend in with the soldier's outline, features blurring, replaced by a swirling mass of hues, colours and shades. The air grew thick and fetid, sending him dizzy, filling his mind with an ever-changing array of images, some he recognised, some not. His mother's face, first laughing, then scowling, his Nan, those eyes so full of concern, Trevor, hands held out, urging him to reach out, and Neville. Hate-filled features, snarling, teeth glinting in the ever-changing kaleidoscope invading his senses.

His head spinning, Ben stumbled forward, not sure where, no longer caring. As the walls returned to solidity, he remembered the lantern and reached down to find that it was still glowing, although weak. Everywhere, everything was as before. Broken pieces of rock, wood and metal littered the ground, water dripped and the blackness pressed in on every side.

In his head rang the voice, forever calm, forever comforting. "It'll be all right, Ben. Move forward."

With his left hand gripping the lamp, he groped forward, until at last he touched the unmistakeable cold, hard metal of a ladder. Elated, he placed his foot on the first rung, and instantly the lantern died. He jumped back in alarm and the lantern slipped from his grasp, clattering against the broken ground. He debated whether to pick it up, but then peered upwards and saw the faint, tiny sliver of daylight and knew he no longer needed it. He climbed, not knowing where the ladder leaded, or even how high it was. All he knew was that this was his only chance.

Chapter Twenty

Gripping the handle of the hatch, for one horrible moment thoughts of the entrance to the shelter flooded his mind. What if rust sealed it tight, just as it did the main door? Heart beating, he pulled. Something gave. A slight movement, a grinding of long unused mechanisms, wrenched from their slumber, screeching their annoyance. He pulled again, the heavy bolt creaked free and Ben cried out in triumph, put his shoulder against the hatch and pushed.

Slowly, unbelievably, the hatch door eased open and the light flooded in. The door swung right over and fell to the side with a clang. He wriggled through the opening and rolled over onto the coarse grass, gulping in the good, clean air.

From a distance came the sound of voices and he rolled onto his stomach, facing their direction. It sounded like Neville and his cronies. They were still laughing. No matter, Ben couldn't care less about any of them now. He closed the hatch door carefully, then cast his eyes around him to try and get his bearings.

This was a part of Darley Dene he hadn't visited before. Some aspects, not so far away, appeared familiar, but others less so. He strained to listen, to pick anything that might take him in the right direction. From the distance, the sound of cars, the occasional lorry, so he wriggled forward and eventually spotted the wall. He hauled himself up and broke into a jog, bent double, careful not to make too much noise and reveal himself to Neville. Better to leave him thinking Ben remained trapped down in the shelter, suffering. The thought made him smile. Poor, pathetic Neville, how mad he would be when he learned that Ben had managed to escape, unharmed.

A second thought took the smile away from his face. Now free from the terrors of that awful place, his mind slowly returning to normality, he struggled to come to terms with what he had experienced. Approaching the wall, he faltered, relief giving way to fear and disbelief – the rejection of what his senses witnessed down in the shelter. Had fear and panic conjured up those dread images, caused him to hear voices, hallucinate? How could any of it be possible, he wondered. Taking a breath, conscious of the others so close, he jumped, grabbed the top of the wall, and hauled himself over. Crossing the road, he recalled the soldier's words. Bitter, angry words. What type of vengeance did he mean?

Nan sat in her room, the clicking of knitting needles a welcome sound and he stood in her doorway, watching. At first, she did not notice, her lips ruminating in time with the almost hypnotic tip-tapping of the needles. The simple normality of the scene brought him such comfort, so much joy that an overwhelming desire to rush over and throw his arms around her welled up inside him, and he blurted, "Nan, I'm back, and I love you."

She gave a little start, turned and beamed. "Oh Ben. I didn't hear you come in. Are you all right?"

She hadn't heard his words. Perhaps that was for the best. An awkward silence fell between them, until he gave a little self-conscious laugh, followed by a nod. "I'm fine."

"Tea will be ready soon. You look awful, Ben. Have you been down to that place again, because if you have—"

"No, no," he lied, but taking a glance down at his filthy clothes, scuffed knees, sodden socks and shoes, he realised how dreadful he looked, and he muttered, "I fell over, but I'm all right. I'll go and get washed."

After tea and a quiet evening sitting next to his nan, alone in his room, thoughts of what had happened kept racing around in his head, making sleep impossible. Usually he drifted away in seconds. He rarely worried. But this was different, so much more intense. The soldier's aura of malevolence, so difficult to forget, troubled him. He tossed and turned all night, strange visions of running, screaming soldiers invading his mind.

A sudden eruption of noise caused him to sit bolt upright in bed, breathless, afraid.

He peered into the darkness. Something about his bedroom had changed, a curious smell hanging in the air, and there, over in the far corner, a faint orange glow slowly grew bigger and more vivid.

In disbelief, he watched as dark, tangled shapes within the glow took on more distinct forms – those of men. Soldiers, darting in every direction, hands pressed against the sides of their heads, wailing in terror. Great blasts filled the air, flashes of light, smoke, masonry falling down, flattening men to the ground, consumed with great mounds of rubble. Others were hurled into the air, bodies twisted into impossible positions, rag dolls flapping grotesquely, helplessly, horribly.

As the room shuddered with each successive explosion, Ben rocked forward and back, eyes squeezed shut, hands clutching his hair, trying to block out the scenes played out before him. A huge blast caused him to chance another look. From the melee of destruction and death, came the face of the vengeful soldier, expression flat and empty, staring at him, eyes black, so pitiless. "Give me what is mine," he whispered menacingly.

Ben tried to scream, to get away, run, but some invisible force prevented him. Muscles refused to work, voice nothing but a squeak.

The soldier rose up, body growing impossibly huge, head thrown back, cavernous mouth emitting the bowel-loosening wail of an air-raid siren, growing louder and louder, filling the room with an intensity of sound.

Lashing out with fists and feet, Ben forced out a scream, which energised him, bringing life back to his body, and he sprang out of bed.

He stood breathing hard, not daring to believe he was in his room again, his own, safe, warm bedroom. A sliver of grey dawn light peeped through the crack in his curtains and he saw nothing had changed. There was his bedside cabinet, his chest of drawers, his wardrobe. It was all there, no falling masonry had flattened it, no falling bombs setting everything alight. Everything perfect.

His heart pounded as he lowered himself on to the edge of the bed. Bending forward, elbows on knees, covering his face with his hands, he sat and tried to make some sense of what he'd seen. Never, in all his life, had he experienced a dream so vivid, so real. More than a nightmare, something else ... Dragging his hands away, he stared into the distance and considered a developing horror – was it a dream at all?

He stood up on legs still wobbly and made his way downstairs to the kitchen. Limbs ached, eyes red raw, his hands shook as he made himself tea and toast.

Sitting at the kitchen table, the first sip of hot, sweet tea brought a certain clarity to his thoughts. A determination to solve this mystery. If it were possible, if it were even true, he knew he had to unravel what was going on. To set his mind at rest, he needed to confront the soldier and wrest an explanation from him – if he could do such a thing. And the only way to do that meant he would need to return to the buried shelter.

He waited for his Mum and Nan to leave for church. Mum had given up trying to persuade him to go well over a year ago, and respected his decision. But perhaps if Mum had invited him to join them this Sunday, he would have agreed. He struggled to understand the meaning of what he'd witnessed these past few days, perhaps some quiet moments in a church might help him disentangle everything.

He could also put off revisiting the shelter until another day, prepare himself.

He could. But he knew he wouldn't.

As it was, Mum never offered, gave him a little smile, patted his cheek then was gone, Nan toddling behind her, checking her handbag for all the things she thought essential for the service.

Ten minutes later, certain they were gone, Ben slipped out the house. He had in his pocket the tiny torch Nan kept under the sink for emergencies. All being well, he would be back before his folks returned from church, but just in case, he left a note on the kitchen table. 'Gone out. Be back soon.' No need to explain further, partly because he wasn't sure of the reasons himself. This was something he simply had to do.

Chapter Twenty-One

A beautiful warm day brought a lightness to his step as he swung into Breck Road. The sunshine gave him the confidence to confront whatever it was he would find down in the shelter and the certainty something, or someone would protect him. The kind soldier had spoken to him, shown him the matches, the lantern, guided him to the ladders. Whoever these ghosts or visions were, they were using him for good. Surely.

He didn't hear them until it was too late. Donna and Francis.

Fifteen years of age, vicious and dangerous, like weasels. They loomed from out of the side entrance of Saint Luke's, swiftly barring his way and cutting off his retreat in one, easy move. They cackled maniacally, the way they always did.

"Where you off to, Ben?" asked Francis, squat, ugly and brooding, his pinhead jutting forward, slack mouth sneering. Beside him, Donna, in sharp contrast to the thick-waisted Francis, stood tall and slim, her long blonde hair falling to her shoulders, her mouth full, the best-looking girl Ben had ever laid eyes on. If she knew how much he fancied her, perhaps she would cease to torment him. The pair of them made Neville seem like a cuddly teddy bear in comparison.

"Somewhere," Ben answered simply. He waited for the voice to come into his head, to tell him what to do. But there was nothing. When Francis circled him, head bobbing, the first tiny tendrils of terror slowly tightened.

Francis tutted, shaking his head, looking at Donna in mock disappointment. "That's not good enough, Ben. You see, we've been talking. Talking to Neville, and he told us all about your little adventure."

Donna suddenly reached out and touched Ben so delicately on the cheek he almost cried out, not in surprise, but in sheer joy. He gaped at her. It was only the briefest of touches but for Ben it said so much. "Tell us Ben."

Lost in the loveliness of her face, he knew he couldn't resist. "Yes," he said, buzzing with the thrill of surrender, "I – I mean *we* discovered some tunnels."

"Tunnels?" asked Donna softly.

"Yes. Huge things, frightening too. Deep under the ground."

"You'll show us?"

Ben nodded meekly, then Donna, taking his hand as if he were a little boy, led him across the road towards Darley Dene.

Chapter Twenty-Two

It was only when they'd clambered over the wall and dropped down onto the other side that Ben noticed squat little Francis wasn't with them. Donna didn't appear in the least bit interested, turning all her attention to Ben, flicking the hair from her face and grinning. Perfect hair and perfect teeth in a perfect face. Ben, mesmerized, felt the heat rising to his jawline.

"Where's Francis?"

She shrugged. "Who cares? Perhaps he got cold feet." She smiled and again ran the back of her fingers down his cheek. "Perhaps he knows how much I like you."

Unable to breathe, Ben's legs buckled and he stared at her in disbelief. "You ... you *like* me?"

"I've always liked you. Now," she took hold of his hand once more, "show me the shelter."

Swallowing hard, he led her towards the entrance.

He stopped at the top of the steps leading down to the metal doors. So innocuous, but beyond a house of horrors. He turned to Donna. "I'm not sure we should go inside."

"Oh?" She produced a bag of sweets and offered one. Ben took it and paused, watching trance-like as she slowly popped another into her mouth. Focusing in on her mouth, lips wet with the sweet's juices, he would rather watch her all day long than do anything else.

Aware of his stare, she chuckled. "You're cute," she said. "I've always thought you were, but just recently…well, you've got better."

"Better?"

"Yeah. Older. You're not a little boy anymore, are you? I like that."

"Thanks," he muttered, not sure what else to say.

She stretched out in the grass, arms cushioning her head. Another smile and she patted the ground next to her. "Come and lie here."

He didn't hesitate and sighed as he breathed in her perfume. To be this close … He craned his neck, allowing his eyes to wander over her slim frame, the thin black bomber jacket, faded blue jeans, pink and white sneakers. The height of sophistication.

"This is a weird place," she said in a distant sort of voice, her eyes roaming across the crystal clear sky. "Especially on a Sunday. So quiet." She propped herself up on one elbow. "Nobody else knows we're here, Ben."

He held her gaze, certain she could hear the hammering of his heart against his chest wall. Nodding, his throat dry, tongue thick in his mouth, he managed a pathetic, "Yes."

A chuckle and she lay back down.

"On a weekdays you can hear the trains in the marshal yard."

"Marshal yard?" she looked at him, frowning. "What's a 'marshal yard'?"

"Where trains move their freight around."

"How do you know about stuff like that? Your dad into trains?"

Ben paused, crunching down on the sweet, making a loud cracking sound as if his teeth had snapped. "I don't have a dad."

"Oh." She looked back towards the sky. "Sorry. Me neither."

"Really?" He perked up a little at this new information. Perhaps she was a kindred spirit and could understand some of his pain? "Did he…I mean, was he in the War?"

She snorted. "Him? You've got to be joking. Nah, Mum says he was invalided out and ran off with some barmaid from New Brighton. I was about two so I don't remember him at all…thank God."

"Mine—"

"Hello there wimpy."

Ben snapped his head around and sat up in total disbelief at the sight of Neville striding towards him, apish grin on his face. Accompanying him was Francis, giggling moronically.

Moving to stand up, Donna beat him to it, grabbing him by the arm. He moaned, staring at her, pleading. "You ..."

"Well, wimpy," said Neville, taking Ben by the shoulder, tugging him free of Donna's hold. "So, you got out then? Must have been dark down there though, eh? Enjoy it did yer?"

Neville let him go, giving him a push for good measure. As he stumbled and nearly lost his footing, Donna placed the heel of her palm in Ben's chest and shoved him over the top step. He careered downwards, desperate not to fall, but near the end he completely lost his footing and smashed into the metal doors, making a deafening crash. Sliding to the ground, defeated, crushed by Donna's treachery, he sat in the dirt and waited for the inevitable.

"Hope you didn't hurt yourself too much, wimpy," said Neville, slowly making his way down the steps, Donna and Francis close behind.

Francis made as if to push past and make a grab for Ben. Neville barred his way and snarled. "Careful, Fran, he's quick with those hands."

"Better use this, then," hissed Francis, pulling out a flick-knife from inside his jacket. He flicked it open and, licking his lips, ran a finger along the evil looking six-inch blade.

Up close, Ben could clearly see how sharp that blade was. He closed his eyes, praying that the voice would come to him and show him what to do. But there was nothing, only the sound of heavy breathing as the three tormentors closed in on him. When he opened his eyes he knew he was truly alone.

It was darker and damper than he recalled from last time. Neville, having wrenched the torch from him, arced the beam across the walls. Francis and Donna held Ben by the arms, having dragged him into the underground shelter with little difficulty. "You try anything," hissed Francis, putting the blade against Ben's cheek, "and I'll stripe you."

"Well, wimpy," Neville said, playing the torch across the ceiling before bringing the beam straight down into Ben's face, forcing him to veer away, squirming but unable to escape whilst in the grip of the others. "This is what we'll do, seeing as you got away last time, spoiled our fun…" He delicately placed the torch on the ground and took from his pocket a bundle of thick twine. He slowly unravelled it. "What we'll do," he said, moving closer, "we'll tie you up, wimpy. Real tight."

As Neville flexed the twine between his fingers, Ben struggled to free himself from his captors, but he failed and sagged in their grip. "Please, Neville," he groaned, all bravado gone, replaced by total terror, "please, I'll do anything, but don't do this. I can't take being locked up in here again. *Please!*"

Neville merely smiled as his two accomplices wrestled with their increasingly uncontrollable charge. "Hurry up," spat Donna, "he's like a bloody little slippery worm," and she kicked Ben in the shin for good measure. Ben cried out and Francis laughed, deciding to give Ben a kick in his other shin. Everyone laughed except Ben, who cried, holding nothing back.

Enjoying the moment, Neville stepped around Ben's back, yanked his arms behind, and twisted the twine around his wrists.

Then all movement and all laughter ceased, everyone freezing, jaws dropping as the shelter reverberated violently with a single, massive crash.

Before the shaking barely stopped, the bombproof shelter-doors slammed shut.

For the briefest of moments, a stunned, preternatural silence enveloped them all. The darkness, malevolent, suffocating, broken only by the tiny beams of the torches, mocked them whilst everyone took in the enormity of what had just happened.

Reacting first, Neville uttered an animal like growl from the back of his throat, pushed past the others and attacked the door with his fists. The others joined in, only Ben remaining still, watching them with detached amusement and he worked his wrists free from the un-knotted twine.

Frantic, the gang of bullies, in an uncontrolled, hysterical assault, pummelled the doors, kicking and raking it with their nails, voices crying out in unison, "*Help, let us out, help!*"

Standing there, a thought developed in Ben's mind. Here was the reason why no voices sprang into his head. There was no need, for locking them all inside was the best defence he could ask for. Who-ever watched over him had a plan, a wider objective, which, as yet, remained concealed, but which Ben felt sure would soon be revealed.

A sudden roar snapped him out of his reverie and he looked up to see Neville striding towards him, face a grim mask of fear, drawn and wide-eyed, a demon, possessed by something beyond his control.

"Who locked the door?" He took Ben by the throat and shook him, ramming the torch close to his face. Ben squinted away. "You better tell me, you wimp, or I'll kick yer fuckin' teeth in."

"Let me." Donna, those pale blue eyes so big in her lovely face, stepped between them, and touched Ben's cheek. "How do we get out, luvey? Please help us."

Ben studied her, eyes unblinking. "I'm not sure I can Donna."

"Let me at him," said Neville, attempting to push past Donna.

She held up her hand, voice not as confident as before, but remaining quiet, gentle. "No, no need for that, Nev. Ben, my angel, you tell me and I'll do whatever you want. We can go out, maybe the cinema, or down to the fair. Just tell me, luvey. Tell me how to get out."

A smile spread across Ben's face. "What, so that afterwards you can kick me again, or push me down another flight of steps?" He pulled away sharply, moving fast, faster than any of them had ever seen. He stepped forward and struck Neville under the chin, then took hold of the bully's wrist, twisting it with frightening strength and consum-mate skill.

Squawking, Neville dropped to his knees, the torch dropping from his hand, the other held aloft, pleading, "Oh God, you're breaking my arm."

Ben stepped back, scooped up the torch and shone it at the others. Donna stood, disbelief written in her wide eyes, her lips trembling with the first signs of fear. "I don't know who locked the door," Ben said, a note of menace in his voice, "but I think I know what's going to happen next."

They stood and looked, none able to comprehend his meaning. Neville, bent double, massaging his wrists, glared but didn't move. Donna, rigid, too afraid to do anything else. And Francis, creeping into the little pool of torchlight, his mouth quivering, his finger coming up to point in disbelief towards an area behind Ben. "Oh shit," he said in a tiny, frightened voice.

They all looked, consumed by bewilderment and fear, at what was happening all around them.

Ben, although a witness to it all before, nevertheless stood mesmerized. The walls churned, turning themselves inside out, becoming an unformed, glutinous mass. Lights, from wherever they were, glowed a sickly orange colour and figures, ghostly, shadowy shapes without real form or density, emerged. Noises accompanied them, the murmur of countless voices, the clamour of leather hobnailed boots on metal floors, and then, most hideous of all, the wail of an air-raid siren, its mournful, horrible sound growing in volume with every passing moment.

The three thugs fell to their knees, hands clamped over their ears, but nothing could blank out that sound. It filled the room, ever louder, ever more terrifying.

Ben alone stood, watching. Ignoring the jabbering trio of bullies, he trailed the torch beam down a long, winding passageway, revealed by the orange lights. He snapped his head round, toeing Neville in the ribs. The big bully's face, streaked with tears, came up, eyes black in skin chalk white with terror. "This way," Ben yelled about the screeching sirens. He stepped forward, seizing Donna by the shoulder, shaking her. He motioned with the torch and repeated his command, "This way, if you want to get out."

She instantly broke into a run, a mad thing without a care for any-one or anything else. Francis stumbled not far behind, crying like a baby. Within seconds, with nowhere to go, they reappeared, trembling and dazed.

Forewarned by its shrill whistle, Ben flattened himself on the ground as a bomb smashed through the concrete ceiling with a tremendous blast, bringing down a shower of plaster and broken bricks upon everyone.

Donna fell, struck by a piece of brick and Francis, coughing, groping around like a stricken Great War soldier overcome with gas, creased himself into a tight ball, and blubbered for his mother.

Terror gripped each of them.

Another blast, then another. Ben barely had time to tug Neville downwards by the sleeve before a subsequent rain of bombs struck home. Amidst the noise, unable to make himself be heard, Ben put his mouth to Neville's ear. "We have to go."

With all his strength, he hauled the big bully along the passage, both of them reeling like drunkards whilst all around them ceiling, walls and floor shuddered from the constant pounding of falling bombs.

Lost amidst the maelstrom, Ben fought to keep his concentration, desperate to pick out any recognisable feature, which would keep him moving in the right direction.

"Move forward, Ben," came the familiar voice, cutting through the thumps and blasts with crystal clarity, "down to the left. Half a dozen steps more."

The words proved true as Ben's hand curled around the comforting coldness of the metal ladder. Unable to resist, he let out a whoop and, with Neville close behind, began his ascent.

Pushing open the cover, he fell onto the ground whilst around him the night air was alive with noise and flashing lights. Neville, emerging like someone woken from a nightmare, whirled, eyes wide with fear, demented, close to losing total control. Ben held him back lest he run off and blunder into a pit, or a mangle of twisted metal. Donna and

Francis, appearing close behind, oblivious to all such dangers, ignored Ben's desperate please to stay still, and ran blindly into the darkness.

"What the hell…"

Ben looked deep into the bully's eyes, took a steadying breath and prepared to speak, then stopped.

The night receded in a blink, the noise and lights fading instantly, daylight regaining control, the distant song of birds the only sound.

Shaking, Neville patted his body and grinned, not daring to believe he was unharmed, that it had all been just a terrible nightmare. Or was it? Taking hold of Ben's arms, he shook him violently. "What *was* all that?" he gasped, barely able to speak.

"I don't know," answered Ben truthfully. "A memory, a message… a warning not to go there again? I don't know what it was, Neville, but I do know we're safe, at least for now. So, come on, let's go."

"Wait." Neville held onto him, and for a long moment neither spoke. Then, at last, Neville mumbled, "Thanks. For what you did." Ben gave the tiniest of smiles. "You won't… *tell* anyone about any of this? I mean, about how I was, down there?" He nodded towards the place from which they had just emerged.

"No, Nev, I won't."

Breathing a sigh of relief, Neville winked, "We'd better get away, before anything else happens," and they broke into a run, made the wall, and clambered over to the safety of the outside world.

Chapter Twenty-Three

The kettle sang as Ben came down the stairs to greet his Nan and Mum, back from a shopping trip. His Mum grinned, and gestured to Nan to go into the kitchen. "Come into the front room, Ben," said Mum.

Sunlight poured through the window, bathing the room in a welcome warmth and Ben flopped down on the sofa, a little on edge not knowing what his mum wanted to speak with him about. Mum took off her thin jacket and sat down opposite him. She leaned forward, looking him straight in the eyes. "Ben. I want you to tell the truth. Honestly, how did you get hold of that photograph?"

Ben turned his eyes to heaven and groaned, "Not this again, Mum."

"No," she snapped, suddenly angry. "I want to hear it from you, the truth. I can't believe you would go through my things—"

"I didn't, Mum. I tried to tell you, but you wouldn't—"

She looked away, not listening to his denials. "I've never seen Nan so angry. She's really disappointed that you could…and I'm – just you tell me. Now."

Realising there was no point arguing with her, Ben's only dilemma was either to tell her the truth, which seemed so implausible, or simply lie. But lies were usually found out, and more heartache, anger and shouting would follow.

He closed his eyes. "The truth, Mum?"

"All of it."

Taking a deep breath, he told her. Everything. The tattoo, how he got split up from his uncle… He looked at her, half expecting her to interrupt, but she didn't. She sat, her mouth a thin line, eyes hard, penetrating. He wriggled in his seat. "I came to this tent and there was a soldier there, sergeant I think… Anyway, he started talking to me about commandoes, Special Operations Executive, and he—"

She gasped, face turning white. "He said that? Those same words?"

"Yes. Then… I can't really remember much after that as it's all a bit vague, but I do remember going inside another tent and on a table, was the photograph."

She sat back, arms folded, one eyebrow arched. "You found the photograph *at the tattoo*?" He nodded. "You're seriously expecting me to believe that?"

"Yes, Mum because that's what happened. Honestly." Her eyes, full of doubt, bore into him. "Mum, I'm not lying. It was on the table. I took it and put it in my pocket when I heard Uncle Brandon calling me. I didn't give it another thought. I put it in the back pocket of my jeans and forgot all about it, until you woke me up that morning, pushing it in my face."

"So, are these the sort of stories you make up at school, is it?"

"Mum, why would I lie? What do you want me to say, that I went into your bedroom, went through your drawers, found it amongst your things?"

"Well that's what you must have done. There's no other explanation, certainly not this stupid, half-baked nonsense you've just come up with."

"And how did I know where to look?"

She thought for a moment, blew out her cheeks, cheeks now red with building rage. "You must have heard a story, or something. From Paul's mother, I shouldn't wonder, so you went through all of my drawers and cupboards until you found it."

It was Ben's turn to lean forward. "Mum, if I'm lying, the photograph won't be there, will it? In your things?"

"What? Well of course it won't, you've got it – I mean *had* it!"

"Yeah, but that's just it – I didn't have your one because I didn't take it from you. I had the one the soldier gave me, at the tattoo. So, go and have a look and find the original."

"Don't be so stupid, Ben, of course it won't be—"

"He's not being stupid."

They both looked up to see Nan standing in the doorway. "Go and have a look. Bring the whole box down. It's time he knew the truth about all this."

Mum clicked her tongue impatiently and got to her feet. She stopped and scowled down at her son. "You've changed, Ben. You never used to be like this, all these lies and stories – I blame those boys you hang around with."

"Mum, please, just go and look."

Another glare, then she pushed past Nan and went out.

Nan sat down and gazed out of the window. Neither of them spoke. From upstairs, they heard the sound of Mum stomping around, opening her wardrobe, slamming a door, then pounding pounded down the stairs. She came into the room, a little breathless, holding a small shoebox and sat down with it on her knees.

"Open it," said Nan gently.

Ben looked from one to the other, feeling the tension, wanting to jump up and delve through the box himself.

Finally, after letting out a long breath, Mum eased open the lid and went through the contents, with great, almost reverential care.

Holding his breath, Ben watched her and Nan looked out of the window. It was as if she knew what the answer was going to be.

Then Mum gave a little cry and Nan spun round. She smiled at what she saw.

She had her answer.

Chapter Twenty-Four

"I met your Dad the night of the big raid on Darley Dene."

They sat around the kitchen table, drinking their tea. The photograph Mum took from the shoebox lay in the middle of the table. It was similar to the one found by Ben when he met the mysterious soldier, but with distinct differences. His Mum's photograph was cleaner, not creased, and focused more finely. It definitely showed the same man, however. Due to the greater clarity of the image, Ben had no trouble identifying him.

The soldier at the tattoo and from the marshalling yard, the one who saved them on the marsh.

Picking it up, Mum studied the photograph, and she smiled as the memories returned. "He stayed here," she pointed beyond the door towards the living room, "on the sofa in there. The next day, he left early, anxious to get back to camp. Later, Nan and me went down and learned about the bombs. The camp took a direct hit. Terrible it was. So many young men, killed, caught like rats down there, in their underground shelter. A land mine went straight through the roof... they didn't stand a chance." She pulled out a tissue from her sleeve and wiped her nose. "After that, we sort of got close. Started courting..."

"Courting?"

"Going out on dates," explained Nan, with a chuckle.

Mum sniffed and carried on, "Before long we... well, we fell in love, I suppose you could say. It was all very strange then, with the war and everything. No one really knew what was going to happen, whether we'd be dead the next day or…well, anything…"

"You don't have to make excuses," said Nan. "Wartime or not, you fell in love and there's an end to it."

"Yes. Well, like I was saying…we became close and … well, you know … Within a few months, he was promoted up to sergeant. Almost straight away, they posted him to Scotland. Not sure where exactly, but it was a very long way away. We wrote to one another of course – I've still got his letters somewhere – and in one of them he told me he was being sent abroad." She dabbed at her eyes with the tissue, squeezed it in her fist and stared. "I couldn't believe it. He couldn't tell me very much, because of the censorship, but he'd undergone special training and was now part of a Commando unit. I tried to read between the lines, but it was impossible to get any more information, or any clues and then the letters just stopped. Nothing, for week after week. He used to write to me about three or four times a week, but then, to receive nothing – I was frantic. And I had something to tell him. Something important. I was pregnant."

Without the merest pause, Ben breathed, "With me."

She smiled, nodded. "Yes, Ben, with you. He was your Dad." Her face crumpled and she broke down, pressing the sodden tissue into her eyes. Nan went over to her and held her close, Mum crying into her shoulders. And Ben watched and the first tear rolled down his own face.

The minutes crept by, the sobs growing weaker. Composing herself, Mum drew in a deep breath. "I got so frightened, I went over to Liverpool, to the local army H.Q. I told the officer on the desk I was having a baby and could they help me, tell me some news, anything…"

"And did they?"

"Oh yes, they certainly did that. They told me he'd been reported as 'missing, presumed dead'. He'd been on some mission or other and hadn't come back. Greece apparently. Or somewhere nearby. They wouldn't say very much. All 'Top Secret' they said. Hah, your Dad, some sort of secret agent. Who'd believe that?"

"I would," said Ben quietly. "Special Operations, Mum. Not secret agent. The man at the tattoo told me. Special Operations Executive. SOE. They were formed to cause trouble behind enemy lines." He rubbed his face. "I thought he was killed in Africa?"

"No. No, he was posted to Africa, but his mission was in Greece. At least I think it was Greece. Somewhere in the Mediterranean I think they said."

"Funny how rumours twist things."

Something past between the two women, an unspoken acceptance of Ben's words, and their features softened. Nan reached over and clamped her hand on Ben's. "I'm sorry, Ben. I shouldn't have said the things I said to you. Why on earth didn't you tell me about all of this earlier?"

"What, that some strange army bloke in a tent in the middle of the night gave me a photograph of my dad?" He laughed. "Would you have believed me?"

Nan shook her head. "I suppose not. Not sure if I'm convinced by some of it even now…" She reacted to Ben's sharp look. "No, Ben, I do believe you, it's just that – well, the soldier. Who on earth was he?"

The question wasn't aimed at anyone in particular, but Ben wasn't saying anymore. He'd keep his thoughts to himself, for the time being at least.

That Sunday afternoon dragged like no other he had ever known. Consumed with boredom, kicking his heels, wandering aimlessly from room to room, wishing there was somewhere to go, something to do. He longed for a dog, but Nan told him more than once that as long as they lived on the main road, they couldn't have one. "It'll be out of that door like a shot and straight under the wheels of a car." Her mantra, repeated every time the subject came up. So, this day like every other Sabbath, he had to make do with his own company.

He threw himself on his bed and his mind slowly drifted away, eyes growing heavy, sleep wafting over him.

* * *

It was night and the sky was a sparkling ceiling of stars. A gentle breeze floated up from the sea, but giving scant relief from the thick, humid air. Shedding themselves of their life jackets, two men dragged a little dingy up onto the beach and hid it amongst some coarse looking undergrowth.

Satisfied, the first man pulled off his Balaclava, and used it to mop away the sweat from his face and neck. He pulled the Sten slung over his shoulder around to his front, checked its action, and dropped to one knee whilst the other man opened up his knapsack. "All there, Harris?"

Harris, closing up the canvas bag again, grunted and together they moved on, padding across the sand dunes.

Soon, the sand gave way to broken, hard ground. Keeping low, they swung over to their right and crouched down behind a small, rocky outcrop.

They squinted into the night towards a cluster of buildings, surrounded by a wire fence. The central building, the tallest of them all, sprouted a long radio antennae from its flat roof.

Adjacent stood a lookout tower, no doubt with direct communication to the nearby barracks. To put it out of commission would smooth their way to destroying the radio room.

Slithering forward on their bellies, they reached the main gate and waited, scanning the area in all directions. If there were any sentries, they weren't patrolling right then. "Stupid bastards," snarled Harris. The other shot him a ferocious glance, flicking his tunic with the back of his fingers. Harris looked away, sheepishly.

The man checked his watch. With the Germans defeated in North Africa, and Churchill's orders to cause maximum damage whenever and wherever they could, all they needed was a distraction.

"How long?" whispered Harris.

"Two minutes."

Harris sighed, readjusting the straps of the rucksack.

They heard it then, the faint but constant drone of an approaching aircraft.

It came in low, a black smudge against the night sky, its twin engines growling loud and ominous. A Bristol Beaufort, banking right as the searchlight in the tower burst into life, and a hopelessly inadequate siren took up its high-pitch whirring.

Tracer bullets cut through the sky, followed immediately by the rapping of machine gun fire. But the bomber arced upwards, dropping its payload. Two stick bombs, tumbling to the ground, heedless of any target. They exploded on impact, with the desired effect.

Soldiers, many of them half-dressed, sprang from various buildings, lights going on, then off, as the men raced towards a corrugated steel shelter. Sergeants and officers barked orders and, in the pandemonium, the first soldier put wire-cutters against the metal fence and cut through it.

"We haven't got long before that sub arrives," said Harris through clenched teeth. The other nodded and Harris hauled back on the severed fence, bending back the metal wires to allow enough space for his companion to slip through.

Both of them sprinted across the compound towards the radio transmitter office. They slammed into the wall on either side of the door. They looked around them. In the distance, men were shouting again, but with less panic now. The searchlight's beam cut through the night, but the bomber was nowhere to be seen, or heard.

With a grunt, Harris eased open the door.

They slipped inside a narrow corridor, lit only by dull, orange emergency lighting. Designed to aid people escape, they formed the perfect homing beacon for the two commandoes, and they moved on, silent as mice in that cramped place.

Ahead, a short staircase led to yet another door. The first soldier went up to it and peered through the porthole window in the centre of the door. Inside, the massed bank of electronic equipment hummed and blinked, and from somewhere amongst the array of knobs, dials and switches, came a flow of garbled voices.

He waited. Waited because there was something else. A uniformed radio-operator, sat with his back to the door, headphones clamped to his ears.

The soldier pushed his Sten around to his back and eased out his black dagger,

He went through the door.

The first notion the German would have had of the commando's approach was when the thin steel blade went into the side of his neck. He jerked in a wild, desperate attempt to fight back, but his life was already spilling out over the front of his tunic as the soldier wrestled him to the ground and held him down until the struggling ceased.

He then stood up and gave a short whistle.

Harris came in and immediately set to work, laying the explosives taken from the rucksack. Working quickly, he was soon finished. He nodded and they both made their way back outside to the fence.

The little *kubelwagon* came from nowhere. The first inkling either man had of its approach was the rumbling of its engine, but neither ever thought it would come straight at them. Nor did they think that the machine gun, mounted across the little car, would begin to bark out a stream of bullets that ripped and zipped around their ears. The first soldier dived, hit the ground and rolled out of the way. He managed to find some cover behind a stack of half broken crates. But Harris was already dead, the bullets peppering him across the chest, sending him reeling to the ground.

Something must have alerted the guards, but what, the soldier had no idea. He brought the Sten around and spewed out his own response as the car accelerated closer. His aim was good, the short, controlled bursts hitting the German manning the machine gun first, followed by the driver.

They were precise, well-aimed, unhurried shots but although both of the Germans were dead, the car kept coming. He barely had time to dive to the side and avoid the oncoming car hitting him.

Perhaps that would have been preferable to what happened next, to what ended his life in such dramatic, unexpected fashion.

At the very moment he stood up, the whole radio building exploded in a great roar of flame and smoke. The timer, set for too short a time, proved a fatal one for the solider, caught in the blast.

But the raid proved successful and the SOE could chalk up yet another tiny victory over the enemy.

The room slowly came into focus and Ben rolled over onto his side, sat up and rubbed his eyes. Looking down, he saw the bottom drawer of his wardrobe upturned on the floor, heaps of lead soldiers spilled all over the carpet. But one remained standing. He got down onto his knees and picked the model up, discovering it to be a British infantryman of the Second World War, holding a Sten gun.

Slowly, more than the soldier came into focus. His dream, and its meaning. The toy soldier slipped from numbed fingers and his eyes filled up. Suddenly he was crying, crying for the death of a father he never knew but had been given the chance to discover.

Chapter Twenty-Five

Ben decided not to tell his mum about the dream, unsure of how she might react. So, he kept quiet, eating his meal slowly lost in thought. Somewhere in the distance, Nan related to Mum all about Mrs. Griffith and the problems with her guttering. Propping up his head in his hand, Ben struggled to stay awake.

Later, in bed, he lay and gazed at the ceiling, knowing he would have to return to the shelter. The answer to the whole puzzle was in there somewhere, waiting to be uncovered.

But he dare not go alone.

With this in mind, the following day he called on Trevor.

Standing in the porch, he listened to his friend's grandma explaining how the whole family had gone to Ireland for a little holiday, 'To visit his mother's relatives.' The hastily planned trip meant Trevor had had no time to leave Ben his apologies for not getting in touch.

Thanking the old lady, Ben came away sullen-faced, dejected, wondering if he had the courage to go back in to that black hell of a shelter on his own. As he turned the corner of Trevor's road, however, he saw that he wasn't going to be alone for much longer.

Neville strode up to him, face set grim. "I've just called at yours."

Ben frowned, wary of the bully's accusing tone. "But I'm not there, I'm here."

Neville let the sarcasm go. "I'm in no mood for your games, not today. I want answers – and I'm not going to take 'no' for an answer either."

"Answers? Answers to what?"

"Are you thick, or what? Answers to what the bloody hell happened to us down there, in the shelter." He puffed up his chest, doing his best to appear brave. "We're going back there."

Ben gave him a measured look. Neville would be the natural choice, of course, as a companion in that dark place. He'd know what to expect. That wouldn't make it any less terrifying of course, but it might make it a little easier. "Are you sure?"

"I'm sure," muttered Neville, not convincingly.

"Don't think we'll be seeing Donna or Francis again," said Neville as they neared the steps which led down to the door. "Doubt if they'll ever come around here again."

"Think they'll tell anyone about what happened?"

Neville shrugged and gave a little laugh, "Who'd believe them even if they did?"

"Mmm, I suppose you're right. Have you got a torch?"

Neville grunted and brought out a large, black rubber flashlight and hefted it in his hands. "Make a nice cosh this would."

Ben looked at him, alarm bells going off in his head as he recalled the last time Neville led him inside.

Neville, noticing Ben's unease, passed the torch over to him before moving down the steps, with Ben close behind.

Inside, it appeared the same as always, the air rank and damp, the walls running with water, rubbish and debris littering the floor. Ben played the torch around, but couldn't pick out anything unusual or different from his other visits.

Moving over to some old rotten boxes, Neville kicked them halfheartedly. They fell apart and Neville stooped down, gathering together pieces of the broken wood. Ben looked on, fascinated, as the older boy wedged the door open with pieces of wood. Dusting his hands, he turned and grinned at Ben. "I'm not getting locked in again."

"Brilliant idea, Nev."

Neville, having finished his makeshift door jam, tugged at the door, checking it could not close. Satisfied, he stepped back and said absently, "You could switch that torch off now and give it here. There's plenty of light coming through the door."

Ben did so. He squinted towards the ceiling, picking out where great blocks of granite, dislodged by the land mine blast, had crashed to the ground. He marvelled at how thick the roof was, that despite the direct hit, it hadn't completely fallen in. "I don't think this is the place where the bomb struck. The men were buried alive. Here, the roof is still pretty much intact."

Neville came up alongside, peering upwards. "You think it's further inside?"

"Yeah, in that weird part where time and space seemed to spin totally out of control." He turned, about to add something more when a great swish of sound followed by a massive shadow enveloped him. Instinctively, his arm came up, but he was too late and the torch cracked square across his jaw. The world went black.

Blinking open his eyes, he cried out as a jolt of pain shot through his face. He waited, without moving, giving himself time to try to understand where he was, what had happened. His jaw throbbed. As he went to lift his hand, to touch the swelling, he found he could not move.

Ben sat on the ground, hands over knees pressed up against his chest, lashed tight together with thick twine. Neville put the finishing touches to the last knot and sat back to admire his handy work.

"Feeling sore, wimpy?"

Ben winced as he opened his mouth to speak and managed only a deep groan. His jaw felt like ten times too big. Sure it was broken, the first tears welled up and he looked towards the grinning Neville in despair.

"I reckon you won't get out so easy this time, wimpy." Neville laughed, rubbing his hands together. He brandished the torch. "This'll last maybe another five or ten minutes before it goes out. Then you'll be all alone in here, because I'm leaving you." Ben moaned. "Yeah, that's right, only this time, you won't be going anywhere. Even if you do manage to get free, you'll be so terrified you won't be able to move. And, guess what, no one will hear yer scream."

Ben attempted to wriggle his feet forward, but Neville's knots proved too well tied. He cursed and spat through his aching mouth, "I'll get you for this."

Neville laughed again, "I don't think so, wimpy. You're down here for good, mate. You see, I've gone and covered over your little escape hatch." Neville grinned at Ben's shocked look. "Yeah, that's right, you heard me. I came here early this morning and blocked it all up. You see, you helping me out of here the other day was the best thing you could have done."

"But Nev," he muttered, mouth barely able to form the words, "please, for God's sake, you can't just leave me here."

"Why not?"

Ben gawped at him. "But...but I'll die."

Neville nodded. "Yeah. Hopefully. If not, I think you'll be driven crazy, being down here in all this dark, with all them ghosts!"

"Nev, please, think about it – you saw it all too. This place really is haunted. Don't you want to know why?"

"Not really. I think you did something. I don't know what, but you've been down here loads of times, that's obvious. You knew your way around, wimpy, and I think you had it all planned."

"Had what all planned?"

"All that stuff you did with the lights and that. It was you. You set it all up, to scare the living shit out of me. And, d'you know what?" He leaned forward, face so close to Ben's he could see the open pores around his nose and cheeks. "I *was* scared. More scared then I've ever been in my life – and you did that to me, you little shit."

"Are you mad? How could I do all that?"

Neville stepped back. "I dunno, hypnotism, some sort of lighting system, or something. You're a clever little bugger and I always knew you were weird, like you was sick in the head or something. But you underestimated me, wimpy because nobody does what you did to me. No one." He clapped his hands together. "Anyway, I'm off now. Have a lovely time… *wimpy*."

With all the talking, Ben's jaw ached too much for him to say anymore and he slumped back against the wall, sobbing gently. Neville laughed, his whole body shaking. Ben, mouth wet with trails of slobber drooling from his lips, mustered up one last appeal. "Please, Neville, I'm begging you, please don't leave me."

"Ah, did-dums." Neville stepped away, head held back, mouth wide open, enjoying the thrill of the moment. "Bye, bye, wimpy." He turned to go.

Without any warning, as Neville took his first step, the ground beneath his feet gave way. Where once there was a scattering of rubble and metal, now a gaping hole appeared into which Neville plunged, arms flapping out in a desperate attempt to slow his descent. He squealed, like a pig, voice high-pitched, receding into the dark depths, full of terror. Moments later came a loud, dull thud.

He'd hit the bottom.

Chapter Twenty-Six

Utter silence fell over everything.

Ben sat still, not daring to breathe. After a moment, senses returning, he tried to move, but again the knots proved too tight. He rasped, in a small, frightened voice, "Nev, are you all right?" But nothing came back. A yawning sickness welled up inside him. What if he were dead?

Realising the enormity of what had happened, he took up a feverish struggle to free himself, twisting legs and wrists. The pain in his jaw forgotten, replaced by another where the bonds cut into his flesh, but he put it out of his mind. He had to get away, free himself. Nothing else mattered.

Ben worked on relentlessly at the twine, gritting his teeth, ignoring the discomfort of his raw wrists. All the while, as he struggled, he became conscious of a growing disturbance from the gaping hole down. A series of stifled moans.

Neville was alive!

Buoyed up by this revelation, the thought spurred Ben on to greater efforts. Groaning and snarling, he kicked out his legs and writhed around as if consumed by agony, and slowly, little by little, the cords loosened.

An unearthly, shrill noise drifted up from the depths of the hole. He stopped and listened. The sound was not human. More animal perhaps, like whimpering dogs, or...Or what? How could dogs be down there, underground? So, rats perhaps. Did rats make such sounds, and so loud?

If some animal were down there, what would it do to Neville?

A final effort and he managed to free his legs, pushing out his knees from the binding with a grunt. Twisting his hands free, he grimaced when he saw the raw welts around his wrists, the blood spotting all along the area where the twine had seared his flesh.

Pushing the burning pain from his mind as best he could, he moved cautiously to the hole and peered down.

It was too dark and he couldn't see. Then he remembered Neville's torch. He picked it up, switched it on and sighed when nothing happened. It was dead. Cursing, he slapped it several times into his empty palm. The light blinked and came on, a thin yellow beam trickling out. He directed it into the abyss.

What he saw below was a scene from hell itself, forcing him to recoil in abject horror, the start of a scream dying on his quivering lips.

He stood, eyes wide, the back of one hand pressed against his mouth, his breathing strained, rattling in his chest. Nevertheless, the desire to see more, to confirm the reality, proved too much and he inched over to look again.

Neville lay, mouth a gaping hole, blacker even than the one he fell into, whilst around him a living chaos of whitened limbs writhed and crawled. Seemingly hundreds of hands, like maggots around rotting flesh, clawed at his body, intertwining with his own limbs, creating a boiling, brimming mass.

From within the seething pile, faces appeared, grossly distorted faces, baring jagged teeth and bulging eyes, necks straining forward, like a many-headed beast of mythology, ashen white and green veined. Ghastly shrieks filled the air, a cacophony of angry cries from black mouths, turning the air fetid, bringing bile to the back of Ben's throat. He retched and tried to look away, but some huge, compelling force dragged his gaze to the pit once more, where he watched those putrid white limbs slowly and relentlessly swallow Neville up whole.

Gasping, Ben tore himself away, staggering over to the wall where he waited, sucking in his breath, trying his best to recover.

Neville was lost and Ben's only thought was to get away.

He turned and felt his bowels loosen. Before him, the terrifying image of the soldier from his previous visit appeared. "I warned you. I will have my vengeance if my needs are not met."

Shaking his head, Ben blurted from thick, swollen lips, "But I don't know what you want!"

"Justice," the soldier hissed, and then receded into the blackness as the shelter transformed once again into how it was on the night of the fateful bombing raid.

The shrill sound of the air raid siren smothered the cries from the pit. Materialising from the ether, a horde of men clamoured around, running in every direction, desperate to escape and find some protection from the falling bombs above.

Ben, nothing more than a blind drunkard, swayed and staggered forwards, the torch in his hand almost forgotten, groping in the direction of the steel ladder, and a chance to make it to the surface.

He remembered then and pulled up sharply – Neville had blocked the exit.

Heartbeat racing as the panic gripped him, his only hope now was to get back to the main door and pray Neville's jams were still in place.

He broke into a run, passing through the many soldiers wild with horror, and when he reached the pit, he glanced down briefly. Neville had disappeared, engulfed by the writhing mass of naked limbs still wriggling and twisting in one seething lump of flesh. Retching again, he swung away and his eyes rested on something in the dirt. Without thinking, he bent down and picked it up. A small, black, dog-eared notebook. He considered opening it, but a tremendous explosion almost knocked him off his feet, and he broke into another sprint and headed towards the main exit, cramming the little book into his back pocket.

He whooped with glee when he saw the open door and spilled out into the night, taking in a great lungful of air, intoxicated with its freshness, its cleanliness

He had no time to relish his euphoria, the air around him filled with the shrill scream of falling bombs and the blasts as they hit their targets. He clambered up the slippery steps, trying to get as much distance as he could from the shelter, from the mounting danger.

At Paul's collapsed tunnel, he threw himself down on his stomach, pressing both hands against his ears to try and block out the noise. He chanced a glance towards the shelter and watched in growing horror the sight of a massive landmine falling slowly, unerringly towards the far side of the shelter, the very place where Neville had fallen into the pit.

Truly huge, the parachute above it tiny in comparison, the bomb floated downwards. Ben marvelled that such a small piece of material could support such a large explosive device. And then, as he watched, it struck and detonated with tremendous force, the night lit up, becoming day for one awful moment. There followed the great roar of the explosion, and the final blast, like a great rush of wind, all seemingly happening at once. He cried out, burying his face into the dirt, as debris, earth and stone swept over him, a tsunami of destruction, blown in all directions by the enormity of the landmine.

Holding his breath until his lungs screamed, Ben waited for the aftermath of the blast to cease. Moments later, a pattering of fallout came down onto his back, like rain. He took his chance and, scrambling to his feet, paused to take one last look at the place where the shelter once stood. All that remained was a pile of rubble, the building itself obliterated, the men inside buried amongst the devastation.

He ran, ran like never before, not stopping until he reached the safety of his own front door.

Chapter Twenty-Seven

In his desperation to get away, Ben did not notice the world changing all around him. Night slowly replaced by day, the many blasts and crashes disappearing into the mists of the past. The present had returned.

Unaware of any of this, dazed, confused and frightened, he pounded on the front door.

It opened and Nan's welcoming face appeared. Ben fell into her arms, sobbing uncontrollably, a stream of tangled words spilling out of him.

She helped him inside and sat him down at the kitchen table, then took a flannel and ran cold water through it. She bathed his forehead, the soothing coolness revitalising him and slowly his sobs subsided.

"Try and tell me what happened, Ben."

He shook his head, breathing through his mouth, lips tender, face tight, painful. Nan went out and returned a few moments later with a mirror. She held it up.

He gasped, terrified at the grossly swollen Halloween mask gazing back at him, a face peppered with cuts and great blue bruises.

She held his hand. "Try your best."

So he did, and this time he left nothing out. She listened as he told her about Neville, how the bully lured him into the shelter and tricked him, struck him with the torch and tied him up. Then the changes,

Neville falling into the pit, the bombs falling. He shifted and pulled out the notebook. "I found this."

Nan opened it, scanning the first few pages. "This is an army pay book, but I don't recognise the name. I'm sure the police will know. You wait here, I'm going to Auntie Kay's."

She left at a run and Ben sat, wondering if he had done the right thing. The part about the soldier he had omitted, thinking it too fantastic for anyone to believe.

He got down, wincing with the effort and gingerly touched his back, where some of the falling debris had struck. Puzzled, he sat. How could hallucinations conjure up something so real?

He lowered his forehead onto the table and closed his eyes, all strength leaving him. His face throbbed like a million tooth-aches and he wished he could just drift off to sleep and wake up with everything forgotten and back to normal. But he knew that no matter how hard he wished for this to happen, it would never become true. Neville was in that hole and something dreadful was happening to him. He had done all he could to save him, but .... There was nothing left to do but wait.

"Everything will be fine, Ben," came a voice through the ether. Ben sat up, instantly regretting it as the pain pulsed through his face. There was no one there, but he recognised the voice nevertheless. The soldier at the tattoo, his soothing voice wiping away all the fear. "They'll find Neville, so don't worry. Everything will become clear very, very soon. Trust me, Ben. Trust your Dad."

Ben's mouth went slack and the tears welled up in his eyes.

An hour later, things did become very much clearer.

Nan, having returned from phoning the police at Auntie Kay's, wanted to take Ben to the hospital. "I don't like the look of those bruises, Ben." But when the police arrived, they insisted that he return to Darley Dene with them. Although Nan resisted, the police were not to be denied so, like a troop, they marched down there, and at the wall Ben showed them how he had scaled it so many times before.

Of course, Nan could not climb, so they left her behind, the two officers flanking Ben as they crossed the expanse of Darley Dene and ascended the steps to the steel entrance door.

Ben paused, uneasy. Things were not the same – there was no sign of any destruction. The door was closed and everything seemed quiet, undisturbed. The police were growing impatient.

"You had better not have taken us on a wild goose chase, my lad," said one of them, a big lumbering man who looked like he left a coat hanger inside his jacket he was so square-shouldered. "Because if you have…"

The threat was obvious, but Ben simply shook his head, jabbing his thumb at his cheek, "Does this look like a wild-goose chase?"

Exchanging glances, the two policemen gave a collective shrug. "Did you dig all of this out?" asked the other, smaller man.

"Well, with some friends, yeah."

"Dangerous."

"And stupid," added the big one, for effect. He eased past Ben, took hold of the door's handle and pushed it down, then put his shoulder to the door and leaned into it. The second officer joined him, both grunting with the strain until, with a grinding groan, the door inched open. Switching on their torches, they stepped inside, Ben close behind.

There was no evidence of any recent damage, just the detritus Ben met on his first excursions into the depths of the shelter. With torch beams cutting through the gloom, they moved forward until an impassable wall of collapsed woodwork and masonry prevented further progress.

"Nothing," said the big one. "This place was cleared during the War, lad. About thirty bodies were brought out, as far as I can remember."

"They sealed it up afterwards," said the other, kicking away at the ground.

"Check the ground."

They all turned towards the direction of the voice. The man who had helped Ben through the marshes all that time ago stood, framed in the doorway, with Nan next to him. He came closer, smiled down at Ben and gently ruffled his hair. "Voices, eh Ben?"

Ben frowned, staring at him in disbelief.

The big policeman blew out a sigh. "If you've any information about any of this, I suggest you tell us what it is."

"Yes, I have constable," said the man and bent down, brushing the flat of his hand across the ground with exaggerated care. "I think we'll find something..." his voice trailed away as he dusted away the thin layer of grit and dust. Everyone watched, breathless. The man's hand worked faster, sweeping away a large area, slowly revealing wooden planks, planks that were for the most part solid and unbroken. But then...

"Well I'll be..." muttered the big policeman.

A little way beyond where they stood, the planks appeared splintered, cracked, then broken. Without any words, they all set to work, pulling up the broken slats, throwing them to one side to reveal underneath a shaft.

Ben groaned. The shaft, or hole, was filled with rubble. He stood up, but the big policeman, crouching down, strained to listen to something. He gave a little start. "Christ, I can hear something!" He gave Ben knowing look. "I'll have to radio in for assistance," he said and he was already making his way out of the shelter, passing Nan, who gave a little smile. "Quite a lad you've got there," he said and she smiled again.

"If you'll all wait outside," suggested the other policeman, "I'll keep watch here, just in case."

Outside, the Sun was high in the sky. It was early evening. They sat down on an old, fallen tree trunk, the three of them, Nan, Ben and the man. No-one spoke for a while until Ben found the courage to ask the question that was burning away inside him. "Voices you said. What do you know about any voices?"

The man looked at him, a smile flickering at the corners of his mouth. "I think you know, Ben."

"I do? You mean...you too...?"

His nod was the only affirmation Ben needed.

"What are you two talking about? Whose voices do you mean?" asked Nan, but neither of the others was forthcoming.

"How did you get in here, Nan?"

"This gentleman showed me an old door," she said.

"The name's John," he said. "You remember that old door, don't you Ben?"

"I do. I doubt if many people know it's there."

John grunted and pointed towards the shelter. "I doubt if many people know about what happened down there either. There's a lot of secrets connected to this old place."

They lapsed back into silence and waited for the emergency services to arrive.

Later that same evening, after Ben returned from the hospital with an all clear, everyone sat around the kitchen table reliving the events of the afternoon.

The big policeman returned with news that the fire brigade and ambulance were on their way. Within fifteen minutes, men worked feverishly to clear away the rubble from the shaft.

Underneath they found Neville.

He lay amongst a collection of broken bones and army equipment, unable to move due to two broken legs, but unconscious anyway. It took hours to haul him out, strap him onto a specially adapted stretcher and take him to emergency.

John, both hands cupped around a large mug of tea, explained. "He landed on what used to be a service tunnel, used by the soldiers to communicate between different parts of the shelter. It took the brunt of the direct hit from the parachute mine and the men killed during that dreadful night remained undetected ever since. They sealed the place up just after the War." He reached inside his jacket and produced the army pay book, found by Ben. "In here are the details of one of the missing men. Soon his remains, and those of his fallen comrades, will be exhumed and given a proper, fitting burial."

Ben stared at the little book without speaking. He recalled the detective coming to the house, to scold him and his 'irresponsible behaviour' over the past few days. "You could so easily have been killed, young man."

"Yes," said his Mum in a quiet voice, "and if he hadn't been so...'irresponsible', those poor men would never have been found, would they?"

The detective had no argument against that and he left, reluctantly giving Ben a pat on the back for all his help.

John left after tea and Ben watched the big man lean towards Mum and kiss her lightly on the cheek. Mum went to close the door, but already Ben had squeezed through, running up to catch John as he set off down the road.

"I need to ask you ... "

John smiled. "I thought so. The voices."

"How long ... "

"They started when I was over in Normandy. I was with the Pioneer Corps. We were making our way inland, with orders to prepare a landing strip for inbound aircraft. We came across an old deserted farmhouse and stayed there for the night. I woke up in the early morning, the sun not yet up, and I heard them. Voices. I could understand every word, even though they must have been in French."

"What did they tell you?"

"The Germans had laid a series of mines across the exit to the old farm. We would never have known. I didn't tell the lads *how* I knew, but I persuaded them to take another route. We probably would have all been killed if we'd gone in the direction we were originally heading for." He pulled in a deep breath. "I heard a voice again ... when I was crossing the marsh. It told me, very clearly, to make my way over to where you were."

"Oh my God....but ... why? How?"

He shrugged. "I've no idea. My old mum used to tell fortunes back in the Twenties. Maybe I've inherited her gift. Who knows? But whatever the reason, I'm glad we met, Ben. You see ..." His face took on a troubled look as he grappled with something inside. "The thing is, your mum and me, we're ..."

"John, it's all right – I know."

"You do? And you're not—"

"No. I'm not. Perhaps that was why the voice came to you when it did. Perhaps he wants Mum to be happy."

John considered this, his mouth gradually broadening into a smile. "You know what, you could be right."

As he got ready for bed, Mum came in and sat down next to him. She held his hand and stared deep into his eyes. "Ben... Please tell me you won't do anything like this again."

Ben smiled and gently laid his hand on her arm. "I promise, Mum. No more digging around underground bunkers for me."

She kissed his forehead very softly and left him alone. He lay there, staring up at the ceiling, going over the events of the day, until eventually the tiredness overcame him. As he closed his eyes, he became conscious of a presence in the room. But he wasn't afraid. He knew what it was.

From the far corner emerged the shadowy figure of his father, still dressed as he had appeared during the evening of the military tattoo. He was smiling. Ben slowly sat up and he was smiling too. But then he tensed as another vague figure appeared. It was the soldier from the shelter. Ben gasped, recoiling, but his father held up a calming hand. "It's all right, Ben. It's all over now."

"You did what I wished," said the soldier, "you laid us to rest."

The last thing Ben could see of him was a large, gleaming smile. Ben relaxed, so relieved.

"I'll always be here, Ben," said his father, growing more vapid, his voice hollow and distant. "Mum is happy too, Ben. She's finally found someone who will care for her, and not disappear." Ben could just make out a smile. "I'm so proud of you, Ben. So very proud. You're my boy, Ben. My brave boy."

A single tear fell down Ben's cheek and he looked at his bedroom wall, where he'd stuck the photograph his Mum used to keep hidden away in a cardboard box in her room. Now framed, Ben reached out and touched it gently with his finger before turning around again for one last glimpse of his father. But he'd gone. Ben knew, however, that his father would always be near. And the thought brought tears. Tears of joy.

Epilogue

A heavy silence hung over them both after Uncle Ben sat back, the story ended.

Henry eyes fell on his uncle's hands, clasped together, the liver spots large, and for the first time he realised that this man, whom he barely knew, had lived a life, known both happiness and suffering, and been brave enough to recount the story of what happened in Darley Dene. Such thoughts brought feelings of respect to Henry, for this man who seemed so weighed down with the re-telling

After a few moments, Uncle Ben stood up, taking away the cups to wash them under the running tap. Henry watched his back. He had so many questions, but how to begin? The story proved a painful process, so Henry decided to wait. At the right moment, Uncle Ben would take up the conversation once again.

The evening progressed and whilst Uncle Ben busied himself with making something to eat, Henry switched on the television and settled down to watch some mindless quiz programme. With little stomach for it, he put his head back on the cushions and let his eyelids close, drumming up images from his uncle's tale.

The clatter of plates snapped him out of his reverie. He sat up, reached for the first piece of toast and marmalade and frowned across at Uncle Ben, settling into his armchair, sipping tea.

"Not eating, Uncle Ben?"

Ben forced a tiny, sad smile. "No. Don't much feel like anything, to be honest."

Looking down at the toast, Henry felt much the same way. Nevertheless, so as not to appear ungrateful, he took a small bite from a corner then took a breath. "Can I ask you something?"

Ben drank his tea, shrugging, "Of course."

"Your Dad..." Ben looked up. Henry waited, uncertain, but there was no aggression in his uncle's eyes, merely an openness, inviting Henry to continue. "Did you ever...ever see him again?"

Ben took a moment, his eyes clouding over. Another painful memory perhaps? "In a sense. When my Mum – your Grandma, died – we all went through a terrible time, Henry. In a way I'm glad you weren't old enough to remember any of it. You were only three months old. She developed diabetes, getting progressively worse over a period of about two or three years. Started complaining about feeling tired, having no energy. Then she took to her bed...never really got out of it again. Dad tried his best, but he was still working full-time back then and..." He paused, holding his face in the finger and thumb of his right hand, biting back what Henry felt sure was a tear. "It's funny, but even though it's over ten years ago, it's still so bloody painful." His hand moved to his eyes, squeezing them.

Henry remained silent, wondering if he'd gone too far. Was this really the right thing to have done, to have forced his uncle to drag up such harrowing events? And for what reason – to satisfy his curiosity. "I'm sorry, Uncle Ben, I never wanted you to—"

"I'm all right," Ben said quietly. "Anyway, she got worse. Doctor didn't do very much. Kept telling her to 'pull yourself together.' Good God...imagine. '*Pull yourself together*'. Well, she did that all right – she collapsed, in the bathroom. By the time Dad called me, the ambulance men were taking her off to Arrowe Park. She never came out. Developed gangrene in her foot."

"Gangrene? Isn't that something to do with rotting flesh?"

"Poisoning of the blood, nerve-endings and the like, yes. Basically your limbs die because the blood supply has been cut off. God, what a choice of words eh? Cut off, because that's what happens. They have to amputate. But Mum wouldn't let them. She refused. I begged the doctors to do something, but all they did was shrug their shoulders."

"What, they couldn't save her?"

"They couldn't go against her wishes. So she died." He looked away.

"My God, that's awful. I never knew about any of this."

"Well, our family has never been all that *open* about all the skeletons…" He chuckled, but there was no humour in the sound, only a deeply entrenched regret. "It's strange, but I keep calling Mum's husband 'Dad'. But, of course, although he wasn't my real dad, as you know, in every sense of the word, he *was*.

"After Mum died, I sat in the waiting room, crying like a baby and my Dad – my *real* Dad – came to me. Just for the briefest of moments. I could sense him, standing there. And his voice saying, "She's happy now, Ben. No more pain." I felt such a warm glow of love in that room, but before I could say a word, he was gone."

Henry pushed his plate away as the last vestiges of hunger deserted him. "So, the man you called 'Dad', he was…?"

"The man who rescued me from the marshes. Your Dad's dad – your Grandfather."

"Granddad John?"

Ben nodded, the smile returning to his face. "He was a grand old man, your Granddad. The hours we'd spend with my train-set. And his stories, from the War…" Another wave of grief. "We all lose what is precious to us, Henry. That's the saddest fact of life. It's not our own death which is so frightening, it's the death of those around us. What we'll miss. Granddad John went into a deep depression after your Nan passed away. Nothing would lift him. I'd sit with him, night after night, took him out on visits, the pub, cinema – it was no good. He just…faded away. Six months after Mum died, he went too – died from a broken heart. But," he perked up a little, "although I miss them – miss them all – I know, Henry…I know…they're here, and they always will be."

Henry didn't need any explanation. Instead, he switched the focus of his questioning. "So, what about the others, Uncle Ben? Trevor, Neville, Paul? What became of them?"

Stretching out his legs, Ben smiled. "Trevor? God, I haven't seen Trevor – for years and years. I met him by chance, ooh, thirty years ago? We arranged to go for drink, but we never did. Don't know where he is now. Paul, the one who was always kind to me... he moved away. Became a solicitor I think. Never saw him again. Donna... she must be – she must be nearly seventy now. Don't know where she ended up but I've often wondered if she kept her looks. All I know is that she moved away, but I've no idea where. Francis – poor old Francis. He was killed in Aden. Joined the army, sent overseas, and killed by some terrorist. We read about it in the papers. Couldn't believe it..."

"A bit like..." Henry's voice railed away. He didn't wish to bring up the subject of Uncle Ben's real dad again.

But Uncle Ben didn't hear, lost in his memories. "The men – the remains of the soldiers we found underneath the shelter – were buried, with full military honours. Very moving it was. A little commemorative plague was put up. But Darley Dene..." His voice grew dark, and Henry frowned, uneasy. "Darley Dene has gone – bull-dozed over to make way for a bloody road."

Henry watched his Uncle, sensing his change of mood, the memories of a lost childhood, lost in so many ways. "And Neville? What happened to him?"

Ben's eyes grew hard. "I hated him, Henry. Always have. I know it's a terrible thing to say... but I just can't help it. He would have left me down there, in that hole, damn him." He looked up at the ceiling, blowing out a loud breath. "Both of his legs were severed right through. He never walked again. Confined to a wheelchair for the rest of his life." Again, that look. "He died a broken and lonely man, Henry. Old before his time, living out his days in a nursing home down in New Brighton and when I read in the obituaries that he had died..." He closed his eyes for a second, "I gave a little cheer, inside." He gently pressed his fist against his heart. "Despite the fact that without him luring me down into that bomb shelter, the remains of those soldiers would never have been found, I still felt such a sense of... satisfaction at the way his life panned out." He closed his eyes again, voice shaking, "God forgive me, Henry, but I could never forgive him for what he did to me."

"It is for God to forgive, Uncle Ben," said Henry. "Sometimes we can't find it in our hearts to do so, but we are not God."

"What did you say?"

Henry glanced up in alarm, afraid he'd said something he shouldn't. "I'm sorry, Uncle Ben, I-er-sort of..." He stood up quickly, feeling anxious. "I think I'd better go to bed."

Ben held out his arm and Henry stood still. "Loss, Henry. It affects us in so many different ways..."

A long moment. Silence. Trembling.

The telephone made them both jump. Ben immediately went over and picked up the receiver. He listened for a moment, turning to Henry as he spoke. "Is that... what, so he's coming home? OK... yeah... yeah, I'll tell him... Are you all right? OK... yeah... bye." He replaced the receiver very slowly. "That was your Dad. It's Grandpa Frank..."

Henry breathed a sigh. "Like you said. Loss."

"No, no, it's not that – he's made a recovery, Henry. He's going home."

"What? But you said..."

Uncle Ben just shook his head, but he was smiling, "Yes, but it just goes to show, doesn't it – you never do know what surprises life will hit you with." His smile grew wider. "And not all of them are bad."

"Is that something your dad used to say?"

"Oh yes." Ben raised wet eyes to the ceiling. "And it's what he continues to say to me ... often."

The End

Dear reader,
We hope you enjoyed reading *Lament For Darley Dene*. Please take a moment to leave a review, even if it's a short one. Your opinion is important to us.

Discover more books by Stuart G. Yates at
https://www.nextchapter.pub/authors/stuart-g-yates

Want to know when one of our books is free or discounted? Join the newsletter at http://eepurl.com/bqqB3H

Best regards,
Stuart G. Yates and the Next Chapter Team

About the Author

Stuart G Yates is the author of a eclectic mix of books, ranging from historical fiction through to contemporary thrillers. Hailing from Merseyside, he now lives in southern Spain, where he teaches history, but dreams of living on a narrowboat in Shropshire.

Lament For Darley Dene
ISBN: 978-4-86750-366-9

Published by
Next Chapter
1-60-20 Minami-Otsuka
170-0005 Toshima-Ku, Tokyo
+818035793528
4th June 2021

Lightning Source UK Ltd.
Milton Keynes UK
UKHW011322180621
385747UK00001B/124